PROMPT
RESPONSES

The East Riding Creative
Writing Group Anthology

Prompt Responses By The East Riding Creative Writing Group.

First Published 2023.

001

Cover and book design by Phil Grainger

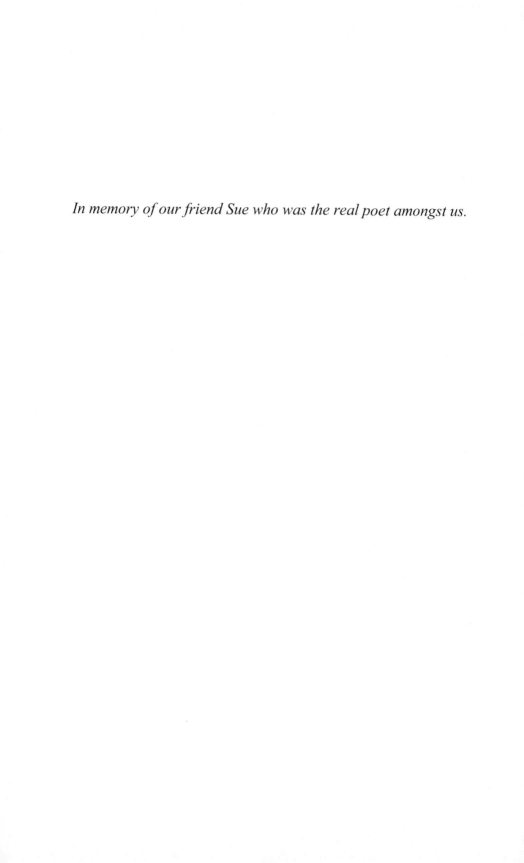

In memory of our friend Sue who was the real poet amongst us.

Contents

INTRODUCTION

The East Riding Creative Writing Group was formed in 2015 when an assortment of people of varying ages and backgrounds, but with a common interest in writing, met at the East Riding Theatre in Beverley to be tutored by local English teacher, writer and performer Sue Wilsea, who has published stories, poems and articles.

That initial course was scheduled to last for ten three-hour sessions, but Sue's enthusiasm and expertise in all genres of writing led to subsequent courses and a sharing of our work, be it in the form of prose, poetry or script. Our growing confidence in presenting our work led to us participate in East Riding Theatre's 'Tale Spinners' competition for amateur writers in 2017 and 2018. We enjoyed success in several categories, which spurred us on to continue developing our literary skills and even following Sues's decision to stand down as tutor in 2019, the group continued to operate with everyone taking a turn at chairing the meetings.

Here we are today, eight years on and still going strong - even COVID couldn't close us down! The membership has welcomed a range of people over the years but the current group has been working together for some time and have become firm friends as well as literary colleagues.

Each month the group chair provides a prompt as a stimulus for a piece of writing to be shared and discussed at the following month's meeting. We have learnt an enormous amount from each other in sharing our work in this way and of course have amassed a huge catalogue of poetry, prose and script, a selection of which we now feel we would like to share in this anthology, entitled of course 'Prompt Responses'. We hope you enjoy it.

THE TALE OF A PAIR OF TRUNKS

Chris Goodwin

It was a cold, gloomy, January day with low leaden skies and no hint of sun. According to the Met Office, the Drearier from Siberia was sweeping through, complete with icy blasts and snow flurries. I was shivering in my study, idly browsing on the computer when I discovered it in all its green, yellow, blue and red majesty: the perfect hammock.

I could just imagine myself lying back, blue sky above, blazing sun; in the shade of a tree, a G&T in one hand, book in the other, swaying gently in a cooling breeze, surrounded with the buzz of bees and tweets of birds.

Before I knew it, I'd clicked.

Reality set in. We had no trees, but I wasn't going to allow a trivial thing like that get in the way.

I found myself all bundled up, sitting in the car, waiting for the heater to clear the windscreen. I had time to kill. No need to scrape.

Then I noticed the workmen – two of them. One was pacing out thirty steps, then digging a hole. The other was following behind, filling the hole back in.

Curiosity overcame me and stepping out of the car I went over. 'Morning, what are you up to?'

Mr Hole-digger stopped and leaned on his spade. 'We're the tree-planting unit from the council.'

I raised my eyebrows.

'We're usually a team of three,' he explained, 'But Sid, he's the one with the saplings, is off sick today.'

I arrived at the nursery when a young lady, fresh out of primary school, asked if she could help.

'I'd like to purchase two trees, please.'

'Oh yes, what type?'

I hadn't actually thought about that. 'Apples I think,' imagining myself reaching up into the foliage to pluck a crunchy apple as I lay back in the sun.

She took me to the tree section. I studied the range of saplings and enquired as to how long it would take for them to grow big enough to supply shade and, maybe, support a hammock.

She told me. I carried out some mental calculations but bought them anyway.

The following Sunday was my grandson's birthday, my little cherub, though to be truthful, more of an imp. He was two years old. We were having a family get-together to celebrate.

I'd wrapped his present up and he toddled over excitedly, chortling loudly, while ripping the paper off. Inside was this green, yellow, blue and red thing. He pulled at it but couldn't get it to do anything, played with the wrapping paper for a while, and then toddled off to find something more interesting.

I could see my daughter giving me one of her long scrutinising, quizzical looks. You know, the one that is questioning whether or not I've still got all my marbles.

I glanced out the window at the two saplings, then smiled across at her.

'Don't worry, love. Put it by for later. He'll thank me one day.'

YOUTHFUL ACTIVITIES

Chris Goodwin

A sad, true account of my limited military training. In later life, as a headteacher, I used to look out of my window as the local army cadets were being put through their paces in the quad. It always used to amuse me no end. It appeared to me that the whole company was made up of the biggest bunch of miscreants, rebels, delinquents and awkward types that we had in the school. Yet here they were in immaculate uniforms happily being marched up and down like happy little termites. This surly bunch wouldn't obey a polite request in the classroom but were deliriously joyous following every loudly barked command to the letter. Human nature is profoundly mysterious.

''YOU GROWING YER OWN GREATCOAT??' The Sergeant Major bellowed in my ear. 'WE'RE NOT IN THE BLEEDIN' GUARDS!! YOU DON'T HAVE TO GROW YER OWN BLEEDIN' BUSBY!!'

With that he proceeded to circle around me, looking me up and down from every angle, regarding my long hair with disbelief, and generally glaring at me with utter disgust as if I was a pile of recently deposited dog poo. Throughout this amusing performance, I stood rigidly to an approximation of attention, trying not to smirk, my right ear still ringing loudly. This was my introduction to the army cadets in 1963 at the rebellious age of fourteen.

I'm still not sure what made me want to try the army cadets out. I should have known. There were no girls and I'd already been chucked out of the cubs and scouts for being 'too exuberant'. Whatever had induced me to give it a go? I think it was probably my

5

best mate who enthusiastically recounted to me about how great it was. You got to fire real Lee Enfield army rifles, SLRs and even Bren guns and there was a camp coming up!

At fourteen I liked the idea of firing guns and attending camps.

Looking back, war seems a strange thing to teach to young kids - very creepy. The military operate in the same way as religion: catch them young and brainwash them. Send us your kids and we'll teach them some discipline! (Along with the subtle art of killing!)

That day I was issued with my uniform, shown how to blanco spats and belt and how to polish boots, buckles and buttons. I wasn't so keen on the thought of having to do all that on a regular basis, or even once, but on a more positive note, we were shown how to strip down, clean and oil a three-oh-three Lee Enfield rifle. That was more appealing. I temporarily put aside my qualms. Take the rough with the smooth.

My general disquiet came more to the fore as we were marched up and down and taught how to turn on the march, stand to attention, dress off and stand at ease, which all felt rather ridiculous and difficult to take seriously. I had great fun winding the young corporal up by moving both arms forward and back at the same time, turning in the wrong direction and being hopelessly out of step with everybody else. It felt like a ludicrous game to me. I remember telling the irate corporal, when berated, that I couldn't help it. I was genetically uncoordinated. He failed to find my performance anywhere near as amusing as I did.

The next week, donning the itchiest shirt, tunic and trousers known to man for the first and only time (a uniform so hideously uncomfortable that it had obviously been designed by sadistic religious zealots), a uniform that rubbed my neck into a sore and brought me out in a rash, I presented myself on parade for inspection.

The Sergeant Major, who I had already established was a very loud man, impressed upon me from two inches away, complete with oodles of spittle, that I hadn't quite mastered the art of blancoing, polishing or ironing and that by next week he was hopeful that I would have grasped these esoteric practices. Except, while proving himself not to be an erudite man, his impressive expletive-ridden rendition was full in equal measures of sarcasm and ridicule, to which, sadly for him, I proved impervious, and fortunately for me, I found absolutely hilarious. A highlight of my brief flirtation with the black arts of dispensing death.

Sadly, despite his cajoling instruction, the mystical skills of blancoing, polishing and ironing, would always, even to this day, prove beyond my abilities.

On the positive side, during my short stay as guardian of the realm I did manage to fire Lee Enfields, SLRs and Bren guns, with mixed success, and go for a week's camp, which resembled a glorified route march with accompanying loud bangs, which I rather enjoyed.

The truth is that I only managed to protect the Queen for a matter of weeks before the Sergeant Major declared that my remaining part of the defence of the realm was likely to be of more use to the enemy than the Queen, and we had a parting of ways. He had finally admitted defeat.

For my part I accepted that I had paid my penance. We had all discovered that the wearing of the hair shirt, accompanied by enforced smartness, ran contrary to my nature. It was time for me to move on.

I don't think I'm cut out for either military institutions or ascetic religious orders.

SOUTH OF EASTER

Chris Goodwin

Mau Rata sat himself down on the couch to explain the events that had been passed down through time by his ancestors.

'The first tribe settled on Rapa Nui, having crossed over a thousand miles of ocean from East Polynesia,' Mau explained. 'Their safe arrival at land was heralded as a gift from the great god Make-make. The gift was perfect – a land of plenty, of water, trees, birds and animals. There were eggs, meat and fruit aplenty. It generated much rejoicing. Life was easy.'

Mau nodded wisely.

'Our first Anki insisted we give thanks to Make-make and honour our ancestors by building the Moai. The massive statues were carved from the volcanic rocks in the quarries and many trees were chopped down with which to roll them to their sites of erection. Much hard work and industry was required, but the gods had to be thanked for their blessings.'

Mau frowned and puffed out his cheeks.

'The life of ease was soon replaced by the toil of construction and transport, but Make-make was content and the ancestors were suitably honoured. Life on Rapa Nui was pleasant and the tribe prospered and grew. Many Anki came and went and always there was the pressure to produce more Moai, for Make-make required appeasement.' Mau shrugged and grimaced. 'And there were times when the rainfall was slight, the harvests slim and hunting more difficult. Make-make took much appeasing.'

'As time passed, the trees began to thin out as more and more were used to transport the huge Moai.' A sadness crept across Mau's face. 'With the thinning of the trees the soil began to wash away and

9

the crops could not grow. The bird and animal populations decreased and hunting dried up, but there were still plenty fish in the sea.'

Mau looked up, his eyes running from one to another.

'More importantly, the water became scarce. Without the trees the rain was not retained. Life became progressively harder.' Mau gestured with his hand.

'The Anki saw this as the anger of Make-make and urged even greater efforts in the making of Moai. Surely, if sufficient effort was put into producing Moai, Make-make would be pleased, the rains would return and bring back the birds and wildlife; life would be easy again.'

'Feverishly the people carved the rocks in the quarries and the last trees were felled in order to move them to their sites. On the day when the last tree was chosen, Hotu Matu'a, the woodcutter, paused with his stone axe, thought for a moment as he stared over the barren surface of their denuded island, and wondered. It was only a brief pause. Wielding the flint axe to good effect he soon brought the very last tree to earth.'

'The last Moai was moved to its position but there were no more trees on which to roll more Moai, so many were abandoned in the quarries and further carving was halted.'

'Now, life was hard and cruel. There was no shade from the relentless sun. Water was so scarce that throats were parched. There were no crops or fruit, no meat or eggs. There was no wood to build canoes or branches to make spears. Fishing became hard. People starved. Then there were roving bands of cannibals to hide from.'

Mau took a big breath, his face darkened with anger.

'In disgust, the people began to topple the statues.'

I CAMERA 2 : IMAGINE A GRAVE
Chris Perkins

Imagine a grave, the shadow of a Victorian church lying half across it. The headstone is new. The inscription is simple, heartfelt; 'mother, friend'. Imagine a lone being, feeling some comfort from dawn's approach.

Let's call him Jim. Of course, it could be Peter, or Harry. We could extend our imagination and move ourselves to another place and we could be witnessing Jacob or Isaiah. If we could develop our thoughts, move elsewhere, there may be Jafar, Pavith, Dhar or Zhen standing there, a small handful of flowers ready as an offering. Were we from a more enlightened mind, Jim may be a Jamima, or Jaghuti or Junko.

But not today. Today we watch Jim. Jim in padded jacket, faded jeans and old trainers. Jim, with less hair than fifteen years ago. Jim with the weight of some other world on his shoulders.

We move closer, detect the slight aroma of sleepless nights and unwashed body. It's early and we hope that Jim will remind himself of basic necessities later. Maybe.

A tear shines against his cheek as it catches in the light.

He kneels. Strokes the dew from the grass as tenderly as if it were alive.

His thoughts drift backwards. A remembered first meeting. A gradual, steady falling. Night of passion. And mornings. Afternoons. The church prompts an unwanted recollection of standing in front of family, friends, God. Promises made. Kept. Kept longer than the first's birth. And the second's. Almost to the third one's.

For some, maybe for Jafar, maybe for Zhen or even for Jaghuti, love lasts forever, never fades in the reality of time. Sometimes ships do sail together on fate's seas, reaching the end port, that final destination, together.

We see fingers dig into the cold earth as Jim recalls a final parting, a refusal to heed pleas and entreating. Ship sailing along different coasts.

Hyacinths, the most purple blooms, selected from his garden, are rested across the soil.

We are close. We can see Jim's chest rise and fall slowly, know that sobs are being stifled. We hear his breath, but are not party to the few words he mutters before leaving.

I CAMERA 1: SHOES 2
Chris Perkins

The opening shot is of the darkest of dark night sky, lingering long enough to allow the audience to marvel at the myriad of bright stars looking down on the humble, almost insignificant Earth. A low discordant murmur from a synthesiser rises and falls, mocking distressed breathing. As the shot pans towards the horizon, a waning moon illuminates the winter scene. A forest looms. To the right, the bright lights and merry sounds of a riotous party can be just heard. A long shot establishes the scene. A large house can be glimpsed, surrounded by a crumbling yet effective brick wall. A broken carriage lies forlorn at the gate, the door opens as if releasing its prisoner unwillingly.

The long shot slowly zooms towards the forest. A disturbance is visualised via the erratic movement of trees and bushes. The sound of an unseen running woman gradually dominates the soundtrack as she breaks branches to push herself through thickets, gasps for air, cries in pain as brambles cut into her skin and tear crudely at the fabric of her dress. The audience is forced to silence.

She stumbles into a clearing. The camera tilts in sympathy. She rights herself, checks behind her for the anticipated pursuer. She's young, mid-20's. Sweat and dirt mix. There's a purity about her and yet the cares of her world have rested too heavily on her shoulders these last few years. What efforts she has made this night to present the best of herself – the flowing tresses, the subtlest almost natural makeup, the most beautiful of evening gowns – all undone in the rush to escape.

A close-up reveals tears welling unsuccessfully from her hazel eyes. A mixture of fear and steely determination illuminate her face.

Fireworks, indicating the lateness of the evening, shock her into action and she heads toward the narrow path leading to her stepmother's modest cottage. In her haste, unbeknown to her, she drops one of the expensive high heels that she has been clutching so lovingly.

As the audience watch her disappear into the darkness, the camera lingers on the dishevelled clearing, the falling snow gradually hiding any trace of her direction.

A new character steps into view. He's not the wide-eyed beast, the scarred-faced monster, the uncaring psychopath anticipated by the audience. He, he is the gentlest of souls. Standing tall, he scans the area. In close up, the softness of his pale skin can be admired. It's flawless, untouched by life's ravages. There's a concern expressed in the worried frowns that trouble him. A close-up of his electric blue eyes reflect the forest scene, as he seeks a clue as to where she has gone. The camera is set at eye level and pans the clearing as if to mimic his desperate hunt, finally alighting on the one shoe.

A final shot of the scene sees him, a prince amongst humans, grab the shoe and squeeze it close to his chest. Looking skyward, the young man mouths a promise that he is determined to honour. As the camera imitates the path of his search, there is a return to the initial shot. The stars come into view, warmer, more welcoming this time.

His thoughts act as the soundtrack - to find the owner of the shoe and offer her his life, his heart and his wish, his deep desire, to marry her – should she be willing.

WANTED

Chris Perkins

The lift door opens and there stand two of the three people in the world that I never wanted to meet. The other is safely in Rampton Secure Hospital, no doubt plotting the revenge she thinks I so richly deserve. The Twins, on the other hand, are here; suited, booted, ties Windsored, silk hankies folded into their jacket pockets. And smiling. Smiling in the way the crocodiles are regarded as smiling.

This is not their area. They prefer the darker, seedier haunts of the east of the city, occasionally drifting into some of the better, classier establishments in the centre, usually accompanied by their entourage of social detritus and a very posh woman who they insist on calling Princess.

This post code is off their well-beaten path. I like working here for that reason. There are always bodies that need a bit of TLC. Always a few that need disposal. To the locals around here the Twins are just some characters that appear in the local paper at times, opening a refurbished pub, or hosting a charity event for a disabled docker. How the pub became so severely damaged or why the poor sod needs such intense treatment is rarely explained by a reporter, they not being as curious as an ex-landlord or the very retired patient.

How they'd found me is a question starting to permeate my hastily thinking brain. There is no easy route out. The Twins guard the lift entrance. A thirteen-flight dash down the concrete stairs will only see me greeted at the exit by one of the boys. One flight up I might have risked a window. But a baker's dozen? There is no soft landing from there, a fact I am hoping not to establish in the near future.

I smile back.

My mind thinks through the previous few weeks. Where had I been? Who had I spoken to? What could I have said? Done? Touched? Which one of my customers might be dissatisfied and just happen to be a second cousin to these two?

'Looking for you'.

They both speak at the same time. On a good day they take turns with sentences. On a bad day, alternate words. I was hoping this wasn't a bad day.

'Saw van.'

I silently cursed my carelessness. In this case, it didn't pay to advertise.

'Your job?'

'You good?'

I look down at my bag of tools, so recently employed, and nod.

'Mum needs'

…..'washing machine fixed.'

I relax. No cash but a favour banked.

THE BATTLE OF TOLSTOY ROAD

Colin Raynor

Harold England and his wife Elizabeth had lived in their house, at number 64 Tolstoy Road, all their married life. They were settled in their own quiet little corner that they would forever call home. But changes were about to occur that would fracture their peace and harmony forever.

Their neighbours at number 66 moved away and a Mr. William Norman, with his wife and six children, descended upon Tolstoy Road.

If it wasn't the constant comings and goings of cars at all times of the day and night it was the terrible music they could hear which seemed at times as though it was coming through the walls. Life became intolerable for the Englands and it seemed the Norman family were 'in their face' all day and every day. That was a phrase that Harold England had heard his colleagues at the Town Hall use, and although he wasn't entirely sure what it meant, it seemed to sum up the situation with their troublesome neighbours.

The only thing to do was to get away for a while, so, although it was only early October, the Englands loaded their caravan and set off to spend a week at Hastings. It really was one of their favourite places and they always parked their caravan in the same coastal field. It wasn't far from where Mrs. England's mother Edith Godwin lived, so they could call and see her from time to time. As they watched the sun settle on the tranquil waters of the English Channel the troubles of Tolstoy Road could have been in a foreign land.

But it couldn't last.

They had to return home, and as they drew up one week later, outside their house, it seemed there was something very different about the place. It was Mrs. England who spotted it first. She was very good at observing things was Elizabeth.

"Harold dear". She spoke quietly but directly into her husband's ear. " Have you noticed that large green vehicle in the front garden of the Norman's house?"

Mr England stopped the car, put the handbrake on and turned off the engine. Not a man to be rushed was Harold England. Stepping out of the car he said, "You are so right my love, and if I'm not mistaken from my Army days, it's a Centurion tank."

"Never mind what kind of tank it is Harold," said Elizabeth, her voice now positively vibrant. "What I want to know is, why that long pointed thing is right across the front of our garden".

"That long pointed thing as you call it," replied Harold "Is the gun carriage and oh dear….."

Harold stopped in his tracks. The small greenhouse, in which he carefully nurtured his plants over the winter months, was just an untidy pile of glass and metal.

"Look, there's a note on the end of that gun thing" said Mrs England. "Are you going to get it Harold, because I'm not touching it."

Harold went and pulled a scrappy bit of paper towards him.

"Sorry about your greenhouse", he read. "Our little son Willie got trapped in the tank and in trying to get out he swung the gun turret to the left instead of to the right."

The note was signed Norman. As he read the note again Harold felt his wife poking him in the arm.

"What is it now Elizabeth?"

"Take a look down the road Harold. Every house in Tolstoy Road has a For Sale notice in the front garden. Everybody's leaving, Harold. We are going to be left with the Normans. What are we going to do?"

"There is only one thing to do, Elizabeth my dear," said Harold. "And it means war."

"I thought it might do when I saw the tank." sighed Elizabeth .

"No, I don't mean because of that. Well I do really. What I mean is, we have to do something before things get out of hand . I haven't worked at the Council all these years without being able to pull a few strings . Before I've finished that lot next door will wish they had never heard the name England."

"Harold, do be careful," said Elizabeth. "You know what the Doctor said. You mustn't get excited. It isn't good for your collateral and you could get one of those pains behind your eye again."

Harold England only half heard what his wife said, although he did think that something she had said wasn't just right. Never mind, he was a man with a battle plan and nothing could stop him now.

It was the following afternoon and Elizabeth England was surprised to see her husband running up their garden path waving a bit of paper in the air. Somewhere in the back of her mind, a distant memory flickered, and then faded again.

"I've got it my dear," shouted Harold.

"You've got what Harold? Do come in before the neighbours see you."

" Neighbours. It's the neighbours this is all about," Harold exclaimed. "It's an Eviction order signed by the Head of the Housing Department himself but it must be served on the family within the next twenty four hours. That's why I've come home to do just that, on those Normans next door."

"Just a minute," said Elizabeth as she closed the kitchen door. "Who do you say signed this paper? Do I know him? Can he do that? Will the Normans take any notice of it?''

"No, you don't know him, as such. I think you met him once at the annual Town Hall dinner and dance. I remember you remarked on his black slicked down hair and his funny little black moustache and the way he kept throwing one arm in the air when he danced. But that doesn't matter now. I'm going round to number 66 this very minute and then we'll see what happens."

"That's what worries me, Harold." said Elizabeth, "I don't think you stand much chance of getting big Willie Norman to do anything he doesn't want to do and that bit of paper, whoever signed it, won't make a scrap of difference to him and his crowd. They are a law unto themselves."

"Well, thank you for your support my dear. What would Wellington have done at Waterloo if all his soldiers had said 'we don't understand French so how can we fight Napoleon Bonaparte?' and then gone home? Anyone would think I was going to my doomsday. No, I've got my battle tactics. Take the enemy by surprise and he won't know what's hit him."

Sometime later Harold returned. To Elizabeth's bewilderment, although her husband was sporting a very painful looking back eye, and it looked as though that important bit of paper had been torn into shreds and stuffed in Harold's coat pocket, her husband had a big silly grin on his face that stretched from ear to ear.

"We won the war, like I said we would," Harold exclaimed.

"But your eye and that eviction notice, or whatever, it's all in bits in your pocket," Elizabeth responded.

"Oh, just preliminary skirmishes before the real brunt of the attack took place," said Harold, with a distinct note of triumph in his voice. "As a result of my joust with the Normans, we move out at the end of the week."

"Pardon me,'' said Elizabeth. "I thought the idea was that the Normans moved out, not us."

"That was the original idea, I do agree my love, but William and I came to an agreement."

"What's with this 'William and I', and what do you mean 'we came to an agreement'?"

Mrs England's voice was assuming a high pitch usually associated with ambulances and Harold knew he had to be careful just what he said next.

"Now calm down, my dear. It's like this. Mr. Norman, William, has agreed to buy our house for the asking price and therefore we will not have any estate agent's fees to pay. Isn't that a good deal?"

"A good deal," said Elizabeth, whose voice had now risen to the sound of a Police car's siren," I didn't know there was an asking price on our house. When did we decide we were going to sell our house, Harold England, tell me that?"

Later still, after a cup of strong tea, Harold explained how he had dealt with the conflict so that peace could be restored again to Tolstoy Road.

"Now you see Elizabeth, this is what happened. You were right. When that Willie Norman has a point to make it is very difficult to dissuade him. He goes for it, straight as an arrow as you might say. And well, the thing is, in every battle you have to know when to advance and when to retreat, making sure that you come away with your pride intact. I didn't let him know that of course. Willie Norman will think he has this day made another conquest. I can honestly say my love, that today I looked that man in the eye, without a single quiver, and that was the end of any further disagreement between us. Now we can go and live in Hastings and see more of your mother as she gets older. You know that's what you really want to do, isn't it?" Before his wife could reply Harold continued.

"I've been thinking for some time that I should resign my position with the council, and I shall now be able to convince them to let me go."

"Have you finished Harold?" enquired Elizabeth.

"Yes, my love," said Harold, still wondering if he had really won the day on the home front, as well as in the Norman camp.

"Do you know why I married you Harold England?

From the depths of his favourite armchair the champion of Tolstoy Road uttered a plaintive cry.

"Why was that my love? Do tell."

"Because underneath that calm exterior you can be so dominant and persuasive and I suppose, as you have explained it all to me, we have really got what we wanted, to get rid of the Normans."

Harold drew himself up in his chair, straightened his tie and thought to himself, thank goodness for that.

"Right well, I think I might just take the dog for a walk to the pub…..." began Harold.

"Oh no you don't," said Elizabeth. "Just you stay there whilst I get something for that eye before it closes up completely."

"Whatever you say my dear. Come to think of it I must sign the agreement Willie Norman and I made. Oh yes, I got it all down on paper . This is a day to remember. A day we should never forget in the history of the England family. Let's see, what is the date? That's it. October 14th·· ' The day we won the Battle of Tolstoy Road."

NURSE BELLOWS' LAST VISIT

Colin Raynor

Granddad knew it was going to be one of those days when the water went off, just as District Nurse Bellows arrived. She gave him a cheery good morning, then went straight upstairs to the bedroom to give Grandma a wash, as she had done so many times before.

"Water's just gone off," shouted Granddad, to the retreating figure of the nurse, and then muttered to himself, "It couldn't have happened at a worse time. First snow of winter last night and now this. Good job I made a cuppa when I got up."

It was a whimsical statement from the elderly sage which the nurse didn't hear, but she had heard Granddad's first call about the water, and it did prompt her to think again about how she could help the old lady. Keeping her warm was the most important thing and so she counted it a small victory when she gently persuaded Grandma to let her take her downstairs to the front room and get the benefit of the three bar electric fire rather than stay in the bedroom where the radiator did not work. Wrapping the old lady in a large towel over her nightdress, she seated her on the couch and went into the kitchen to tell Granddad of her change of plan, closing the front room door behind her.

The absence of water was going to test her ingenuity, but she was determined to do her best for the old lady. Maybe Granddad could help her to remedy the situation.

Standing at the kitchen table the nurse looked the old man in the eye and said to him "Do you know where your stop cock is?"

Granddad just stared back at the nurse, and then with a slight tremble to his voice said "Now then, just a minute young lady. Don't you be asking me about such things. When you get to my time of life you don't think or talk about that ….anymore."

Nurse Bellows wasn't sure if the old man was being totally obstructive or even a little bit crude, which she frequently came across in many of her older patients, particularly the men. She supposed he might not have heard what she had said, so raising her voice, just a bit, but not wishing to upset him further, she asked him again.

"No, I mean, there is no water coming through the taps and they do tell us to check the stop cock. Is yours under the sink?"

"Oh I see. I thought …. well. Under the sink you say. You must be kidding me. That is one place I do not go," replied Granddad. "My back won't let me get down there and our lass has so much stuff under there, if we took it out, we'd never get it back again."

Nurse Bellows decided this line of enquiry was getting her nowhere.

"I'll just go and get my paper out o' room whilst you're sorting out the water," said Granddad, moving from his kitchen seat towards the front room door.

"No, you won't my lad. You just stay right where you are," instructed the nurse. "I haven't started Grandma's wash yet."

"Well, you're taking your time today, aren't you?"

"Yes, but haven't you heard me saying about the water?

Oh, never mind she thought to herself and went back in to see to Grandma, leaving Granddad looking more than a little bemused.

With the lights not on and the curtains drawn, of course, it was dark in the room. The electric fire had warmed the room and the old lady looked very comfortable under the towel.

"Come on my dear we'll just have to do the best we can today." said Nurse Bellows, as she closed the room door and went to attend to the old lady on the couch.

It was at that very moment, the nurse reflected later, that she realised Grandma would not be needing a wash that day or any other day from then on. Grandma's little towelled body was lying silently at rest on the couch and the nurse knew the old lady had breathed her last.

"Have you managed?" asked Granddad. His voice, and his question, were sufficient to make her aware of what she had to do next.

She had to return to the kitchen and speak to the old man. But what could she say to him? How could she tell him that his life's partner had just gone from this world without a word of goodbye to him? He was going to be so upset . What could she say to him? She opened the door and took a few steps towards the old man.

"Mr Grimes," she began. She had never used his name before and perhaps that alerted him to the fact that something was not just right.

"Mr Grimes," she began again, "I'm sorry to have to tell you we won't need that water for the wash". Her voice faded away and she felt tears pricking her eyes.

The old man stood up and walked around the table to the side of the nurse. With a kindly look on his face, he put a gentle arm around her shoulders.

"You know lass, you will have to learn how to stop softening the blow. Come on now. Just tell me straight. She's gone hasn't she?'

"Yes, but how did you….?"

"Never you mind that now. Just you get on that phone and make what calls you need to make when this kind of thing happens. I'll just go in and read the paper to my wife. She likes to keep up with the news."

As Granddad closed the front room door behind him, Nurse Bellows heard the first gurgle of the water through the pipes as the water came back on.

JOURNEY TO JERUSALEM

Colin Raynor

I have a recurring dream about the game that has been known in our country for years as musical chairs. Each time it is the same game, in the same place, but there are subtle changes in every dream.

Musical chairs. It's a children's game of course and when the dream begins that is where I am, back in my childhood. I am eight years old at the annual Christmas party, held, as always, in the village hall that has been the focal point of the community during the previous six dark years of conflict in the second World War. The party starts at five o'clock with a tea, which to our young eyes looks unbelievable, and probably to the adults is unbelievable considering the strict rations everyone is on. Afterwards the children receive a present from under the tree and I feel sure that it is my Granddad dressed up as Father Christmas, but I don't tell anyone..

Then in my dream it is time for the games. Quiet ones at first, 'Simon Says' and 'sleeping lions', but soon it's time for the game we call 'musical chairs' to begin. Someone starts playing a piano although it doesn't really matter if we know the tune because the music will stop abruptly and there is a mad scramble to sit on a chair. That's when I find out how sharp girls' elbows can be, as they unceremoniously push me aside to get on a chair. My friends Peter, John and Mary all join in and they are desperate to win. I don't ever remember winning at musical chairs.

This is where any sense of reality, if there ever was any, becomes somewhat blurred as the dreams continue. Each time I'm sure the noise level gets higher and higher and everything goes faster and faster as the game goes on and it becomes just a bit frantic. I notice there always have to be twelve chairs put out and by the nature of the game adjacent chairs have to face opposite ways. I must find a chair when the music stops. Am I pushed out of the way when I might have been just about to sit down? In my dream I'm determined to carry on. I know I will never win the game but I must keep on trying.

This dream becomes a regular feature of night times during my teenage years and persists over many years beyond. There is no rhyme or reason to when the dream will appear again in my subconscious. I do not enjoy the dreams but must endure this strange nocturnal party. I realise at one point that Peter and John are no longer in the game and I don't recall them losing their seats. It is also around now in the dreams that I begin to have an uneasy sense of the macabre about the whole thing. Each time in the dream I ask myself why this and why that? Has it gone darker in the village hall, or is it just my imagination?

Constant in each dream now are two men I don't know. They stand at either end of the chairs to take one away when the music stops and place the remaining chairs further apart...

The person banging away at the piano is now playing so quickly and producing such a noise I can hardly breathe as I dash around to make sure I'm able to get a chair...

In my dream now, one of the adults is dressed like a Roman soldier, and to my horror I'm sure I can see blood dripping from his sword. Somehow I know he has been involved in the disappearance of my two friends, Peter and John.

When I dream again my eyes are drawn to the other man. He is in a black shirt and on his chest he has a large iron cross. He has a peaked cap and is standing tall with his right arm pointing upwards. I look at his left hand and shiver as I see he is holding a whip.

Then comes the night when there are just two chairs left and only three people running around to the music. Mary and I have been joined by a young man who looks familiar, and yet he is a stranger to me.

We are all three staggering around the chairs and I can just make out that Mary and the man have big yellow stars on their backs. I know I have one too!

Now in my dream, there is no music and I have a real sense of fear. Will it be a child or the man who wins the contest? Then I realise the rules of the game have changed and in my dream I am no longer in the game, just an observer.

It is now I sense, rather than see, that there is no sign of my friend Mary.

The man is sitting on a chair, fastened with ropes so he cannot move, but his head is bowed and there are whip marks on his body.

The same dream comes back, but infrequently, and always to the same point; the man is alone. The only light is from a star in the sky.

In the next dream, I'm not in a room anymore, but on a hillside. Then a cloud obliterates the star and I am left feeling deathly cold and an intensity of deep sadness within me. The dreams end and I know the game is finished. Everything is finished and I am bereft and alone.

Will I find an explanation? Is there one to be found? Do I need to know?

Sometime later, one sunny afternoon, I am driving my car along a country lane and listening to a discussion on the radio about children's games. The speaker tells how some games and rhymes can relate to certain times in history. Ring a ring o' Roses refers to the time of the Black Plague in Europe and how it could easily spread when people sneezed.

Then the man's voice comes out of the radio and informs me that the game we know, in our country, as 'musical chairs', is known in one European country as 'Journey to Jerusalem' and that country is Germany.

THE DOOR IN THE WALL

Daphne Gale

It had rained steadily on the first day with heavy grey skies; not what she had expected at all and echoing the sadness and depression which was the constant companion Maggie had come to Italy to try and escape from. She had taken the one bedroomed apartment advertised in 'The Lady' magazine for three months, hoping the change of scenery and climate would lift her spirits and give her new purpose. Armed with paint pads and art gear, she was full of good intentions to get on with the work her editor was pressing her for, illustrating the flora and fauna of the region and writing up her notes before beginning the text of her Botanical Painting book of the Mediterranean.

The flat was charming, small and simple, the drawback being several flights of stairs from street level beside a corner shop selling basic groceries, but the reward was a tiny balcony overlooking the street and well worth the climb. Looking out over the hill town terracotta rooftops, Maggie could load her plate with crusty bread and a selection of cheeses and olives from the shop below, pour herself a glass of local red wine and enjoy the evening when the skies finally lifted as they had done yesterday, revealing far away mountain tops set against a scarlet and gold sunset. As she sat there, the bell in the convent tower further along the street began to toll.

On her arrival, Maggie had been rather disconcerted to begin with on finding herself next to a convent, but had come to like the sound of the bell which was almost on the same level as her, tolling at different times of the day. Although not religious, she found it oddly comforting, and comfort had been needed after losing her husband Dan in a fatal car accident, also causing the miscarriage of their unborn child. She had found the past year very difficult to deal with,

31

but there had been a silver lining to her grief; enough money from a life policy to comfortably enable her to turn her attention to her career and continue as an artist and writer.

This morning was bright and clear, the skies deep blue and the warm air promising a spell of good weather. A pair of soft beige doves had decided it was safe to sit on a ledge nearby, while she fed them the crumbs from her breakfast croissant. She had set up a worktable on the balcony with her art materials to get the best light and she sat there studying the jar filled with wild flowers which she had gathered on her walk on the path below the town. As she sipped her coffee thinking of starting on the red poppies which she knew would flop and go limp very soon, her attention was drawn to the old door set in the street wall below, opposite. Maggie had noticed it before, of course, and sketched it briefly as the heavy carving, set with iron work hinges and studied crossbands, had drawn the eye.

She wondered if it belonged to the convent and if so, what lay beyond. Did it lead into sheltered cloisters or a secret garden where the nuns could sit in contemplation?

Today, something looked different; the door was slightly ajar, just a few inches, and from the angle she was sitting it was impossible to tell what lay beyond. It was no good. Curiosity got the better of her. She downed her coffee cup and placed the flowers in the shade. She would just pop down and have a quick peak. It was still early morning, and the street was quiet.

As Maggie approached the door, she could now see a squashed cardboard box full of old clothes, maybe left there for the nuns to distribute to the poor. As she bent down the better to see, she heard a sound. Was it a puppy or kittens? Pulling aside the grey material, two dark eyes looked back at her, and tiny starfish fingers reached out. Maggie gasped. It was a baby, a new-born naked baby, beginning to whimper as she gazed at it.

After gently replacing the cloth, she ran down to the main door of the convent and hammered on the door with her fist. The iron grill opened and one of the sisters peered out at her. Then things happened fairly quickly. The nuns took the box with the baby wailing weakly now into the convent. One of them, Sister Agnes, explained they would make enquiries in the town and try to find the mother or someone who might know who it belonged to. The baby would be cared for and if no one was found she would eventually be passed on to the small orphanage belonging to the convent. As Maggie had found her, she could, if she wished, visit the baby and help with its care.

Maggie did wish, and later that day she was allowed to sit in the courtyard beyond the door in the wall and hold the baby girl, and when the nuns asked her to suggest a name, she instantly said Maria after her mother, at which they nodded approvingly. Later that night, as she turned out her lamp and lay in bed, she was strangely comforted to think of those little dark eyes staring appealingly at her. Due to her actions the child would have a chance in life and, who knows, she might even be allowed to continue to have contact and care for her, but she also felt sad thinking of the woman who had been so desperate as to leave her baby there. With the image of the baby clutching tightly at her fingers, Maggie found herself pondering over the consequences in life which sometimes can result from random actions and settled herself to sleep looking forward to the next day in a happier frame of mind.

DAD'S CHAIR

Daphne Gale

For years Dad sat in his chair,
I glance at it waiting for auction,
Can almost see him sat there,
I shudder and look away.

Sad to see the silver teapot going for a song
No one wants such stuff today,
It's just meltdown value, who has tea from a teapot
I ask myself, anyway?
The Royal Doulton vase has gone cheap.
The Beswick horse the next lot,
Not a bad price, a collectable of course
Mum's brass candlesticks do well
Nice, twisted stems, I knew they would sell.

All the while that chair, nudging my brain
The memories just waiting, jostling,
To come back again.
Bad tempered old sod, Oh I know he had cause,
Wracked with pain where his leg was,
Lost that in the wars.
He claimed to be a hero
Should have had a medal he said,
Saved some men in the trenches
Never knew the true story
Mum said, 'Don't ask, just get off to bed'.

Oh the cut glass decanter next, that should do well
Nice silver collar, no damage, mum's pride and joy'
Sat on the sideboard, nothing in it, but what the hell!
She came from a good family of course
Knew what's what, middle class
Privileged childhood, even had her own horse.
What on earth was she thinking, changing her life,
To say Yes to that Ass!

Course now I know the truth,
She was caught, just a lass,
Sweet-talked by a soldier, who happened to pass.
Grandpa said marriage, it had to be,
And so off to the church, and the result was me!
All the good stuff has gone now
Her jewellery too, what bit she did have,
I kept the pearls Granma gave her
To wear as a bride
'tho I don't like to think of her, stood by His side.
And so it's come down to this, I've sold the house
Too many memories, some good, mostly bad
I'm off down to Cornwall, a new life for me
Need to forget my bad tempered old Dad.

Here at last his chair, lifted,
A true Windsor, the auctioneer reckons
'What will you give me for this?'
The computer screen beckons
The gavel comes down and I blow it a kiss

Relieved it's all over, can't say I care
Some other bum will sit now, I'm free of it at last
But I still steal a glance, to make sure he's not there,
In that bloody old chair.

FINDERS KEEPERS

Daphne Gale

A story about childhood in a time of war.

Grey socks slipped down around skinny ankles, in shabby hand me down boots, Jack climbed up the heap of rubble, his keen eyes searching here and there for treasure. He was only seven and slightly built but a tough little runt. He had to be with four older ones in the family to feed and his dad in France, or somewhere, he wasn't sure where. The last time Jack had seen him, he remembered staring at khaki legs in big boots and a heavy hand which patted his head saying, 'Be a good lad little un, for your mam.'

But that seemed a very long time ago and since then the bombs rained down every night crashing and banging. He'd got used to creeping in the cupboard under the stairs with his sisters, Peggy, nine, and Sara who was ten and the bossy one, and it was quite cosy really with a couple of old quilts and a few cushions, a bit like camping he supposed. He knew from talking to the boys at school that they were doing the same, so it was the accepted thing to do. The big boys in the family, Roy and Alan, had dragged the heavy kitchen table into the hallway and slept under there wrapped in blankets with their mum. The really exciting bit was seeing his pals in the streets on his way to school next morning and hearing where bombs had landed, bringing down buildings and even still smouldering in places. Piles of rubble and broken furniture lay around which were usually roped off to allow the wardens and aid workers to get on with their work.

He had learned to keep out of their way, but where it was possible to scavenge, there were pickings to be had. An old biscuit tin with a picture of a white Scottie dog against a plaid background was one of his first finds; it now contained his treasure. Two slivers of shrapnel, a bent silver spoon and some green glass beads on a length of broken chain he thought might be gold.

Jack kept his treasure trove on the narrow shelf at the side of the gas meter in the under stairs cupboard. He intended adding to his hoard until he reckoned he had enough to indulge in the business of 'swapsies' with the other boys at school. Competition was fierce to come up with unusual finds. At present, as one of the younger ones, he was only allowed to hover at the edge of the circle of boys at playtime, as they emptied their pockets and inspected the latest loot, but he could bide his time and told no one about his ambitions.

His mam had told him many times it was dangerous to climb the rubble heaps, but she really had enough to do, queuing each day for bread and walking down to the allotments to see if there were a few veg going spare to put in the soup pot, without watching over him, and as many little boys know any hint of danger is an attraction to be investigated.

Last night had been a bad one. No school, as it was Saturday, so he was free to explore and turning into Morton Road he could see that several houses had not survived the bombs. The emergency services were still there damping down the fires. Jack was determined to be a fireman when he grew up. He knew he could climb the long ladders and couldn't wait to wear a helmet, so he did like to watch them. But, at present, he was more interested in the pile of bricks and wood which had been a cottage behind the hedge nearest him.

It was when he squatted down to inspect a piece of broken pottery with a picture on it he thought he heard something. He listened. There it came again; a whine followed by a slight whimper. Cautiously, he tracked down the sound to some bricks at one side with spars of wood. Lifting one gently, the whimper became urgent. Hardly daring to breathe, and as gently as possible, Jack scrabbled an opening in the rubble and now he could see the bright eyes and dusty whiskers of a little dog staring up at him. He knew he should call a warden and shouted out to one in the street as a little pink tongue licked at his fingers. Quickly removing as much as he could, he was able to free the

38

trembling animal which wriggled in his arms licking his face in excitement as he hugged it in his jacket. Although it was grey with dust and dirty, Jack could tell it was just like the Scottie dog on his treasure tin.

'Oi, come away now lad. We need to get in there', said a voice as rescuers arrived. 'Get back over here while we see if anyone's alive under that lot.'

Jack sat over by the fence with the little dog in his arms while the men set to work. Eventually it became clear that the one occupant of the cottage, old Mr Grayson, had not survived and a stretcher covered by a blanket was carried to a waiting ambulance. The dog whimpered and became excited trying to scramble free. 'Tek him home, lad will you? I reckon he needs looking after and as you found him I think he's yours!'

Jack carried the trembling little dog home tucked inside his jumper.

'Mam, mam look here!'

'What you got there for heavens sake?' Her heart sank. Not another mouth to feed. But she stooped to caress the little animal.

'It's my treasure,' he said. 'He's been bombed so can we keep him? Look it says on his collar his name's Bobbie. He's like the dog on my tin. The fireman said he needs a new owner, and as I rescued him, he's mine. Please mam, please. I will look after him. He can watch out for rats in the yard and our Alan can get bones from the butcher after he's done his delivery rounds'.

Mary looked at her son's earnest little face. How could she resist? He was a good lad, and the dog would give him a purpose instead of larking around the bomb heaps and getting into bother. He saw her smile and whooped with joy.

'First things first, I think he needs a drink and then I'm going to brush him clean'. Off he went, the dog trotting at his heels, already the best of friends.

FIGHTING THE INANIMATES

Doug Douglas

The battle commences sometime around six,
Inanimates spoiling my life,
Most *folk* are OK despite some odd tricks,
But it's *things* that cause havoc and strife.

The first task is on to get legs into pants,
But the garment will surely impede,
Inside out, outside in, in some kind of dance,
Downside up, front to back, I'll succeed.

With both legs in one side, Nil One is the score,
Inanimates already on top,
I struggle to balance and one thing is sure,
All I can do is just hop.

I'm reminded of Peter, our union Shop Steward,
With a 'hop on' one summer morn',
Bounced out of control, truly well skewered,
Through the window he fell to the lawn.

Lucky to live in a ground floor apartment,
Pete wriggled and hopped back inside,
Pants re-arranged for the budgie compartment,
Restoring a bit of lost pride.

Back to my own early morning exertions,
Cursing and hopping in pain,
Much too early for kinky perversions,
Inanimates drive me insane.

So, one leg extracted and correctly located,
My pants now fit rather snug,
But socks can be trouble, can't be placated,
So no time to start feeling smug.

One will go hide and turn inside out,
It's partner hooks on my big toe,
I heave and I stretch and awaken my gout,
But the bugger just will not let go.

They're on the wrong feet but too late to swap,
Just hope no-one looks at me there,
Now into the wardrobe to get a clean top,
A sense of great danger, 'Beware!'

Opening the door with some trepidation,
I hope for a mood of compliance,
But clothes hangers work with vile aggravation,
My efforts repulsed with defiance.

They live by mob rule, the gang on the rail,
My trousers are clamped or just draped,
Attempts to remove one are destined to fail,
But I'm lucky, a T-shirt's escaped.

Now bored by the mayhem the hangers provoke,
They conspire to widen the score,
Gently tilting side-ways they think it's a joke,
As my clothes are dispatched to the floor.

Shaved, showered, dressed, ablutions completed,
Still under relentless attack,
Inanimate objects will not be defeated,
I try my best to fight back.

Flexible things, would be useful you'd think,
See the Hoover with retracting cable,
What's holding me back, it's developed a kink,
Tipping over two chairs and a table.

The hosepipe can reach all parts of the garden,
When drawn to its fullest extent,
It gets trapped, no more flow, the dry soil will harden,
More energy wastefully spent.

I open the gate, push it back leaving space,
To get shopping bags in from the van,
At the very last second it slams shut in my face,
No good reason, it's just 'cos it can!

There are so many *things* that set out to screw us,
But *people* can add to the mess,
Pious car users, disabled bay abusers,
Litter louts, ticket touts and the rest.

We live in the country of nonsense,
Our leaders are right out of touch,
They feel no concern or conscience,
Their value to us, well not much.

MPs, CEOs, Heads of Trusts, Union bosses,
Establishment, untouchables, the elite,
Not a clue what to do about financial losses,
Or to care about those at their feet.

This country is blessed with natural resources,
To use for creation of wealth,
Now it's condemned by 'tree hugging' forces,
Making things bad for our health.

We are the mere mushrooms knee deep in the 'firt',
Only told what we're allowed to believe,
But we are still here, in spite of the hurt,
It's maybe not time yet to leave.

ALICE IN NETHERLAND

Doug Douglas

Alice Robson, Senior Lecturer in Sociology at a northern university was facing a dilemma. She was fighting the onslaught of Multiple Sclerosis. Whilst not yet fully disabled, she did use sticks and occasionally wheeled supports. The mainstream medical world had little to offer her in the way of treatment but there was a growing consensus that cannabis in various forms could help sufferers by slowing the progress of the disease and giving comfort 'in other ways'.

Alice had a certain status to uphold. She had made the right moves with individuals to facilitate smooth progress to her current position. She was now promoting herself in the right places for the Head of Department position which would shortly become available. She was not particularly effective as a lecturer but made sure that her seniors in the pecking order believed that she was. She supplemented her claimed academic achievements with the suggestion to her superiors that promoting a semi disabled but skilful performer in academia would be 'right on' and fully PC.

Under these circumstances, Alice could not ask her students for the cannabis or even try to find their 'dealer' but she fabricated a plan, not just to obtain the drug but to further her career at the same time. She convinced her employers that she should undertake research, fully funded of course, into human behaviour within the 'Red Light District' of Amsterdam. She was aware that this area which tolerated, nay promoted prostitution, also had many outlets for drugs.

Alice was an affirmed 'Ms' but she had a long time would be suitor who could easily be enrolled as her accomplice on a 'Dutch Dash'. This was a bargain break from Hull operated by North Sea Ferries, two nights in a cabin on board and one at a discount hotel in the city. Simon was thrilled to be invited and saw this as a reward for his determined but so far unsuccessful wooing. One Friday they set sail.

A shared cabin presented Simon with hope and Alice with a challenge. They enjoyed a fine meal, Alice encouraging Simon to imbibe plenty of wine. They ventured to a variety show performed by the crew and rounded off the evening in the casino. Feigning exhaustion, Alice rebuffed Simon's romantic approaches.

Disembarking at Rotterdam, a coach tour took the couple across the bulb fields and to the Delft Pottery. Simon purchased a souvenir, a jewellery box which Alice really admired and praised its fine detail. She was disappointed to learn that it was not a 'lever' towards Simon's longed for proper 'coupling' but was a gift for his Mum.

Next, the guide on the coach broke the news that their hotel had been overbooked. An alternative was sought whilst the driver continued with a makeshift extended tour. The outcome was an extraordinary piece of good luck. They were to stay at the Amsterdam Hilton. To Simon's chagrin and Alice's relief they were allocated single rooms. But there was yet another surprise. Their stay coincided with the 25th anniversary of the famous bed-in by John and Yoko. Everywhere was Beatle themed, with the hotel foyer having a mock up of Abbey Road with the famous pedestrian crossing and effigies of the Fab Four. Simon was delighted with this situation and spent the evening watching tribute bands. And Alice was advised by the hotel not to venture out on her own. So, still no 'Wacky Baccy'.

There was no official tour on the Sunday so the unlikely pair wandered through Amsterdam and eventually strolled into the Red Light District. The atmosphere was friendly, with scantily clad young ladies posing on balconies or hanging out of windows offering exotic and erotic services to the passing tourists.

Some premises had windows painted with psychedelic colour schemes. These were the 'brown cafes' that Alice had overheard her students talking about. She explained to Simon that part of her research involved the availability of drugs, so they entered one such establishment. The room was not crowded but there were several tables with young people engaged in friendly conversation. Most were smoking rolled up cigarettes. Alice and Simon asked to join a couple at a table with spare seats.

Never renowned for reticence, Alice was straight in with "What's that you're smoking?"

Smiling and talking somewhat laconically, the lad said, "It's called Northern Lights and it blows your ******* mind man!"

Alice despatched Simon to the bar for coffee. To add to the order Simon pointed to some cake on the counter.

"Two portions please."

"Oh no Sir. It's not real cake. It's hash."

"Never mind the cake, give us the real thing," came a loud insistent voice from behind. Alice demanded cigarettes and the immediate attention of the manager.

Expecting trouble, the manger appeared and sat in the seat which had been Simon's, relegating him to a distant corner.

Alice was forensic in the interrogation of the manger, asking which types of 'smokes' from a menu he introduced would have health benefits, which would induce a 'high' and of course which would 'blow your ******* mind'.

Simon bought them each a cigarette, lit them and started to inhale. Simon coughed and wheezed gaining no benefit whatsoever. Alice drew hard on the fag, began to tremble, slowly stood up, discarded her sticks and walked unaided to the bar.

Simon was left wondering why he had gained nothing from the smoke, but enjoyed some time in mystical conversation with the couple who were high up in the Northern Lights.

Alice was of course absolutely delighted and was able to walk back to the ferry. This was to be a new beginning for her and possibly a different life for Simon.

As they left the ferry on arrival back at Hull, Alice had a surprise for Simon.

"I have wrapped your Mum's jewellery case. I'm sure she will love it."

EVENTFUL HOURS, REAL OR UNREAL
Doug Douglas

Caught in a summer storm in the Moray Firth, Jamie, a lone fisherman, steered his boat '*Capability*' into Lossiemouth harbour, moored up and sought refreshment and hospitality.

He found a warm reception in the dockside pub, 'The Steamboat', and enjoyed the delights of local produce.

Haggis, neeps and tatties were washed down with 'Twenty Shilling' beers, rounded off with drams of distinctive Speyside malt whisky.

His mellow mood was enhanced by the sounds of guitars, banjos, accordians, cajons and earnest voices singing folk songs and sea shanties.

This happy hour of music and mirth was abruptly terminated by the wail of a lone piper heralding the end of the night's entertainment or maybe the end of the world, and certainly an end to Jamie's pleasant feelings.

Driven out of 'The Steamboat' by the mournful sounds of the bagpipes, Jamie found the late evening air pleasantly warm, the storm long abated.

It was after midnight but the northern skies were not fully dark, still light enough for a walk along Spey Bay.

Below his feet the white sands were lit up by myriad sparkling gems from the sky above. This would surely be an opportunity for some serious stargazing.

Walking steadily along the foreshore Jamie sought a spot to pause and look skywards. Approaching what appeared to be a derelict lighthouse, he was startled by strange activity. Suddenly a strong beam of light flashed from the top of the building, focusing on him, stopping him in his tracks. The light was extinguished almost instantly and was replaced by a weird figure; the bagpiper in full flow, the output of noise searing through the night.

How did he get here? Is he a ghost? Was the player in the pub a ghost? Jamie was confused and scared.

He looked round to confirm only that he was on his own, save for the piper atop the lighthouse. He felt compelled to approach and climb up to challenge the noisy intruder. Slowly, as he ascended the spiral staircase, the hideous noise grew louder until the place shook violently.

As Jamie emerged at the top, the piper jumped over the edge and plummeted to the ground below. The wail, so shrill and fierce at first, faded to silence. He was relieved to be free from the noise but felt anxious for the demise of the piper.

Glancing apprehensively at the sky, Jamie saw some shapeless green figures seeming to dance around him. They were the Northern Lights, (not the 'wacky baccy' potions that 'blow your **** mind man) but electrically charged particles emanating from solar storms. Jamie's bewildered mind registered them as ghosts. Hesitantly, he returned to ground level and looked for the piper.

But there was no sign of the piper or the instrument of audio torture. The sands showed only his own footprints, otherwise the beach was clean, bright and featureless.

Jamie was faced with a dilemma. Should he return to Lossiemouth and report the incident or should he continue his walk along the bay? There was no sign of any other human being and no movement except the twinkling stars and the animated green creatures.

So he shrugged off his anxiety as far as possible and continued his walk, crossing the River Spey with all its whisky connotations. He was truly alone with the stars.

His isolation was suddenly shattered by the sound of an aircraft approaching. He knew it was a warplane, probably a Tornado or

Typhoon, but very low and very loud. It passed overhead only a few feet above him and appeared to land not far inland. Jamie remembered that Lossiemouth was the most northerly active RAF station with craft sited permanently on stand-by with engines running, ready to intercept Russian aggressors.

This last hour had been so eventful with emotions ranging from fear to amazement and exhilaration but Jamie was beginning to tire. He turned to make his way back to 'Capability' and catch up with some sleep before reporting his experiences to the harbourmaster.

The walk back to Lossiemouth harbour was without incident and Jamie climbed aboard his boat, pleased and relieved to be re-united with her.

He fell into a fitful, troubled sleep which was disturbed and terminated by an excruciating noise. It was not the dreaded, possibly recently deceased bagpiper, but a flock of greedy incontinent seagulls.

They flew in mobs at 'Capability' depositing guano all over the craft, diving to search for scraps of residual fish. They stamped their feet and stabbed their beaks on the cabin roof.

Jamie rose, showered and shaved in the excellent harbour facilities, and went to the harbourmaster's office. The harbourmaster listened patiently, providing Jamie with mugs of tea whilst he recounted his nocturnal activities. After Jamie had spoken for an hour, the harbourmaster suddenly raised a hand to stop him from continuing with his account.

"I must advise you that your story makes no sense at all. The only lighthouse along the beach at Spey Bay was demolished forty years ago in a controlled explosion to avoid being a danger to low flying aircraft. A bagpiper sounded the last rights as the building crumbled."

Jamie was dumfounded, acutely embarrassed to have his experiences dismissed and yet he had no doubts in his own mind about his eventful journey under the stars.

He sailed on the evening tide, out towards the oil rigs which had invaded his traditional fishing grounds and which occasionally had provided extra work for *'Capability'* as a support vessel.

Jamie looked back and there on the coast stood the lighthouse, the piper on top in full flow.

MARTIN AND JEAN
Graham Bailey

The morning light pushing through his Primark curtains is what wakes Martin, but it is the sensation at the top of his leg that rouses him. A phenomenon he has not felt for a long time. He lifts the duvet and looks towards his feet but the hard boulder that forms his stomach obscures the view. Interlocking his fingers, he clamps his hands across his breast, following the memory of his mum's instruction, to resist the urge to touch. He lies, counting the cracks in the ceiling and pondering her mantra.

"I don't know how you will survive when I'm gone,"

Martin's mum died, three days after his thirty second birthday. Fifteen years of discipline and he started drinking heavily, stopped washing and started smelling.

Now, needing a strong cup of Typhoo to get him back on track, he rolls out of bed. A tee shirt and jeans provide cover, warmth, and a comforting hammock for his belly.

"Oh damn! I'm out of tea bags."

A resolution to reduce his drinking has led to an over consumption.

Revulsion at the body in the mirror causes Jean to look away. Runs and ridges of fat create horizontal flaps reminiscent of a well-used candle. She turns away sharply and scoops up the flesh hanging in front of her. Once fastened, the bra makes everything look normal: firm, buoyant and almost youthful, providing you look whilst not wearing your glasses. Obeying her usual routine, she has a small glass of vodka before adjourning to the café for breakfast.

Stepping into the Rovers Return Café, Martin feels the warm blanket of bacon-laden air wrap around him. There are just two people inside, at opposite ends of the room. His favoured table for regular lunchtime visits is empty so he sits and calls out an order to Rosie. Ten minutes later she delivers tea and a full English.

"You'd better be quick. This is Jean's table every morning. She'll be in soon and you best not cross her. Oh-oh! Too late. She's here now."

The woman who enters looks at least fifty, but could easily be older, and with enough girth to easily occupy two chairs. At least she will not cause a repeat of this morning's issues. She sits down at the other side of the table shouting as she does: "I'll have my usual Rosie...You do know this is my table don't you?"

"Yes, Rosie said, but I always sit here."

"I'm in a good mood so I will let you stay. Just this once, mind."

Jean seems to take to him and she natters away, hardly giving space for a reply. She knows everything about last night's soaps and all about the Royals. Some of her stories about the bald one and the ginger one are new to Martin who listens intently, enjoying himself. Then between them the Sun crossword is completed, fully and quickly, with her allowing him first chance at each clue. A true meeting of minds, perhaps. As the morning progresses, a flock of discarded mugs gather at the table's edge.

"Another cup of tea?" Jean asks. "My treat."

"Oh, erm, I might have had too much. Oh, go on then, thank you, yes please."

Martin watches her at the counter and thinks: short, fat, greasy and a little neglected, but she is good company.

Jean looks over to the table and thinks: short, fat, greasy and a little neglected, but he is good to talk to and safe. What's more he's probably a similar age to what Nigel would have been, which is nice.

All thoughts crumble as the door crashes open. A young girl whose hair has at some point been fastened up in an 'I'm out to pull' style, but is now showing signs of failure, enters. Her dress is typical of a fashion only a striking twenty-year-old could wear comfortably. Tight cream denim jeans and a thin plain white top cut to the waist in a wide deep V. It leaves no doubt that she's not wearing a bra and that at this moment she is rather chilly. Martin's eyes are transfixed. He shuffles uneasily.

Two mugs clunk onto the table. Spilt tea pools into droplets on the greasy surface.

"I used to dress like that, creating never ending fury from my dad," Jean says to break the silence. "It certainly drew the men. That was when I had boobs to be proud of and not spaniel's ears…Dad said it would invite trouble and he was right. It did. He also knew that's what I wanted."

Ruminating intensely does not fabricate the right image. The visualization that does resolve is one Martin would rather not retain.

"She should have a coat on," is all he says.

The girl takes her cappuccino to a far quiet corner and the atmosphere is more relaxed.

A realisation reflects on Martin's face. She is desirable but unavailable, whilst on the other side of the table, Jean is available, good company but undesirable.

Minutes later Rosie arrives with two small pieces of Quiche Lorraine.

"I couldn't resist the smell," Jean explains, "My mum used to make them."

She pushes one towards Martin. "They remind me of my dad."

Martin starts to question, but she continues quickly.

"When dad was ill, towards the end, we were sitting by his bed and could smell baking. He asked my sister to get him a piece of mum's bacon and egg flan. She came back empty-handed saying, "Sorry, but mum says they are for the funeral.""

He erupts involuntarily, rocking backwards on his chair. The laugh is louder than polite, louder than necessary and disturbs all conversation in the café.

"Is that really true?" he chokes, "It's the funniest thing I've heard for years."

"Some of it is. I just wanted to put a smile on your face…"

Her hand drops onto the back of his. The table pushes hard upwards preventing its escape. Sitting quietly, his mind races. He thinks for a moment, sensing an opportunity. How much does company and conversation matter? How much should you be prepared to sacrifice?

"Are you alright? You look a little depressed." Jean presses his hand; "We need something to revitalise you…"

"Have you ever been to the bingo?"

GUARDING THE BRIDGE

Graham Bailey

Jävlar Kuk! My feet and my legs they hurt. My cytokerotin will be rotting in this water. Standing here up to my Knas {shna}, I mean knees, for the past twelve hours, is too much. The stones dig into my soles and drive me to helvete. This bridge is too low. It crashes against my head if I stand up and as I turn, the walls scrape my nose. Why is it always me? I know really; I'm the only one that is not a posh boy. It's the price they make me pay for belonging. Just because I went to a state gymnasium while they were sent to private schools. Attending Epsom or Uppingham, paid for by rich parents, does not make them superior. My friends warned about coming south, said I would be seen as inferior, but I can't accept that, have to try to be equal and thus have to accept their rules.

That thin, young, weedy get, sorry I mean goat, I'm telling this story in English, which is not always easy, that crossed the bridge three hours ago is the only living thing I've seen. He conned me with lots of kinnet, sorry I mean cheek, about his bigger brother who would be following him. He should have been my dinner. I still don't understand why we need to keep them out. The grass is plentiful, and our few measly sheep don't need that much. Hunger is beginning to quell the pain of standing, but even so, I'm going to grab the next goat by the throaty and eat him while his blood is warm.

If I wasn't so cold, grabbing him would have been easy but all I could do was block his path. After he'd explained about his skin condition and delicate wasted muscles, it seemed only right to wait for his father.

It's not nice when parents are so aggressive. We had just started talking when without warning he charged at me shouting.

57

"What big eyes you has got… You freak."

Then my pain peaked as his horns split the cornea causing copious, thick warm liquid to ooze down my face. His tormenting continued. I felt only the air rushing past as he butted me over the bridge rail. Something broke as I landed.

Now my legs and arms won't move and stones push into my back and shoulders. Water cascades around and over me. Stinging wounds seep blood into the water, probably turning it red. I do not know, I cannot see.

Why does everyone think us trolls are aggressive and ugly. We deserve more consideration. At least in the children's cartoons we are multi-coloured and smell of strawberries, rather than pig skit. {skeet}.

SPOOKY CHILLS

Graham Bailey

From the kitchen Julie's voice dissects Paxman's starter for ten, instantly losing me points.

"Come and listen to this."

As I walk in, she's kneeling with an ear to a cupboard door.

"There's a rat in the fridge. I can hear it scratching."

I listen. Sure enough, there is a noise, resembling fingernails on wood.

I respond doubtfully, "It's coming from the door. The rat would have to be in the space behind the decorative panel."

"Maybe it is. I've heard that mice can squeeze through a hole the thickness of a pencil."

As I swing open the fridge door, it crunches against the wall. Daggers leap from Julie's pupils. The light snaps on, illuminating most of the interior.

"There's no sign of your rat."

Suddenly, a teeth-jarring rasping noise rises from behind the crisper and the light fades to black. Julie's tension increases.

"Oh, my God, what's happening?"

"Nothing. It's the safety system cutting in because we have the door open."

"What have you got in there?"

Julie stutters, "Just the usual, plus: a few tomatoes, some full cream, a veg curry and a freshly plucked chicken from Market Barrie."

'None of them would scratch the door."

"The chicken still has its feet. They would scratch."

"Yes, but it's dead. This is getting silly. Close the door and we'll have a drink."

Julie stands and pushes the door closed and we both move into the hall.

Behind us the fridge door springs open, and a cockerel crows.

EXTRACT FROM THE JOURNALS OF THE RIGHT REVEREND JAMES FORRESTER

Janet Musil

James Forrester, Bishop in the Diocese of Northumberland, died in 1902. At the time of this extract, he was the recently-appointed vicar of St John's Church, Templeton, Northumberland.

20th February 1845

I returned safely to the vicarage yesterday evening, following a pleasant week visiting my mother in Oxfordshire. The journey was long and tedious, lacking in event apart from a disturbing conversation I happened to overhear whilst on the road between Northampton and Leeds.

As I embarked, I saw that my coach was occupied by a grubby and malodorous old man, a pedlar of some type; his presence was not long to be tolerated, as he alighted at the first stop along the high road, leaving me in the company of two demure-looking young ladies who huddled together on the opposite seat.

From beneath their lowered bonnets, two pairs of pale gray eyes flicked occasionally in my direction. Neither of the ladies spoke. After twenty minutes or so, the rocking of the coach and my early start from my mother's house caused me to close my eyes.

After a few seconds, one of the ladies, the elder I surmised, whispered: "Perhaps it is safe for us to speak now, sister." The younger must have conveyed her assent as her sister continued.

"I know you are disappointed."

The younger one replied in a slightly louder and more agitated voice. "Disappointed? You are the mistress of understatement. I am angry. Furious!"

The older remonstrated with her sister to be quiet. I kept my eyes closed and, in fact, feigned a slight snore in order to convince my fellow travellers of my lack of attention.

The younger sister continued in a hardly less audible whisper: "We have been treated with the utmost disdain by a man with a fraction, no, none of our talent, a man who deigns to make judgments about our work, based on no other qualification than that he has edited and published a handful of mediocre books."

Naturally my curiosity was spiked by this intercourse, and I retained therefore a pretence of slumber.

"How dare he?" the younger girl continued.

Her sister now spoke again. "He dares because he is a man. By virtue of his sex, he has been granted from birth the natural privileges of the male which convey upon the bearer all the rights, assurance and confidence which we are denied. He thinks we should go home and sew."

The younger sister seemed to shift her position and veritably spat out the following words : "I will not go home and sew. I will not allow him to decide my destiny. I know that my poems have merit, whatever he says."

"Of course."

"And I know that I have a novel within me which will shake the literary world out of its complacency."

"Your anger is justified Emily," her sister responded (and here I had difficulty in suppressing a snort.) "But we must direct that anger in the practical pursuit of our goals. That is why I believe we should reconsider our idea…"

"But why should we?" Emily, as I now knew her, cut in rudely. "Why can we not publish under the names our parents and God gave us? Why must we practise this subterfuge?"

"Because as females we are treated with at best condescension, at worst with derision and hatred. Writing under male pseudonyms, we will be considered, accepted, perhaps lauded. Our books will sell and be read. Isn't that what we want?"

"Oh Charlotte, I don't know what I want!" Emily shrieked petulantly. "My sense of injustice is too recent and raw. How I detest this damned society!"

At this outburst I was compelled to open my eyes. The two sisters immediately shot me startled looks. I turned a disapproving eye on Emily, who returned my glare with what can only be described as defiance – an unattractive trait in anyone, but particularly those of the fair sex. Emily's eyes shifted downwards and appraised my ecclesiastical collar. Her eyes narrowed and then rose to meet again my steadfast gaze. I expected her to issue some sort of apology. None was forthcoming.

As a man of the Church I felt it my duty to address this errant creature.

"Young lady," I said. "Your vile words do you extreme discredit. You show the lack of judgement of your youth and your sex. May I suggest that you listen to the wise words of your adviser, take your….materials, the content of which one can only guess at, and return home to activities more suited to your position."

Emily held my gaze, her eyes full of a deep and ugly mistrust. Charlotte's gloved hand stretched across and was placed upon Emily's knee. The three of us glared at each other. Not another word was spoken and, thankfully, the two women disembarked at Leeds.

THE LETTER

Janet Musil

I'd been working at the Dirty Dime Bar for six months when I got the letter that changed my life.

The bar was one of those narrow, long, underlit establishments that are two a penny on downtown streets. In the evenings it filled up with office workers and guys off the construction site over the road, and then, when they had dragged themselves home, groups of young people tanking up on cheap beer and cocktails before they hit the nightclubs.

I was one of three bar staff - 'my girls' the manager, Stephano called us - who worked six nights a week from five pm til one. Or at least it was supposed to be one – often I was still there washing glasses, wiping tables and refilling the soft drinks fridge at two in the morning. I knew I ought to tell Stephano it wasn't right, but I'd lost jobs before when I'd done that.

This April evening was a slow one. For a start it was a Monday – always quiet - it was drizzling, and someone said there was a big football game on TV, so only a handful of die-hard regulars were crouching on bar stools, hugging beer bottles and every now and then engaging in desultory conversations.

Around seven o'clock I was pouring out a shot of bourbon for old Sam, when a middle-aged woman entered from the street door and stopped, peering into the Dime's dingy interior. She looked across and made eye contact with me and I nodded back at her. She wore a smart cream rain mac and court shoes and looked oddly out of place. She had no bag but was holding a white envelope in front of her with both hands, like a landlord coming to demand rent arrears or a bailiff delivering a notice of eviction.

The woman walked purposefully across the greasy stone floor and stopped opposite me at the bar. She held up the envelope, which was addressed in large florid writing to 'Stella'.

"That you?" the woman asked. She fixed me with a hard glare and I wondered if I'd met her before.

"It is," I said warily, "do I ..."

The woman didn't answer but deposited the letter on the damp bar in front of me, then turned on her heel and left, as quickly as she had come in.

Even though I knew I was going to get into trouble, I picked up the letter and opened it, turning away from the bar. The sheet of paper inside was thin, pale blue and lined. I unfolded it and began to read.

'Dear Stella, I'm hoping my wife has done the kind thing, tracked you down and given this to you. I guess if she hadn't, you wouldn't be reading this. So, I know it's cowardly of me. I should have told you the truth years ago. But now you must be what, 21, 22? and I guess you'll have learnt life isn't always an easy road and people are flawed. I think that's how you spell it.

Anyway, the fact is, I'm your Dad. Sorry to be so blunt, but what can I say? You knew me as Uncle Harry, that nice guy who used to come round on weekends with bunches of flowers for your mom and candy and toys for you. Even took you both to the beach once in a while, and to a couple of Christmas shows.'

I became aware of the floor travelling away from my feet, and the sounds of the bar dulling. Somewhere I heard a voice calling "Another Budweiser over here sweetheart!" but it had no pull on me. Old Uncle Harry, with his brown slacks and his sensible windcheater and his NYC baseball cap – he was my father. Jesus. I hadn't seen him since I was about 12, when he'd simply stopped coming round. My mother had never mentioned him again, but when she was on her deathbed, just before my seventeenth birthday, she'd seemed to want to tell me something, - nearly had - but I'd thought it was something insignificant, like where she'd hidden her jewellery, or the secret ingredient in her famous Lasagne.

I read on, my hand shaking.

'I'm sorry that I suddenly dropped out of your life, but Marlene, my wife, found out about you and your Mom and for the sake of my marriage and my two boys, I had to cut off all ties.'

I leant heavily against the counter to stop myself from crumpling to the floor. Two boys? That meant I had two half brothers. In the space of a couple of minutes my family had trebled in size. Or only doubled, since, skimming through the paragraphs, I realised my Dad was dead and had left me money in his will. A lot of money – 20,000 dollars, I saw, my heart pounding.

"Hey, let's have some service down this end!" one of the customers called impatiently.

" Not now! " I shouted back and then, throwing up the bar gate, I rushed across the room and out the door and onto the glistening sidewalk, scanning left and right, up and down the street. Then I saw her – Marlene. She was standing in a shop doorway a block away from the Dime Bar, watching me.

AT THE PORTAL TO A PARALLEL UNIVERSE

Janet Musil

Nefertiti leaned back on the couch and popped another grape into her mouth. It really had been a lovely day. With Stella away at a tennis tournament and most of her friends out of town, for once she'd been left largely to herself – to walk on the beach, read a book, do a little online shopping and enjoy a long foamy bath.

It was still only seven in the evening.

TV77, she said out loud, and the local news channel burst into life on a floating display. As usual the headlines were about riots in the Eastern Outlands, and further damage to space tourism due to the economic downturn. Why follow the news, it only depresses you, she could hear Stella saying.

Off, Nefertiti commanded. She yawned languidly. She looked around the room.

You there, Zee? She called.

Within seconds Zee was at the side of the couch, head slightly bowed, arms in front of her.

Hello Nefertiti. How can I help you?

Nefertiti turned round on the couch to look squarely at Zee. A Mark 3.4 android, purchased only a month ago and still under warranty. Pricey, but worth it for the extras, Stella had assured her.

Suggest an activity Zee, Nefertiti said.

Sure, the droid responded in her purring voice. Knit a scarf, sketch a bowl of fruit –

Knit a scarf? Nefertiti laughed. Why?

Zee resumed her catechism. Admire the sunset, write a poem…

Stop, Nefertiti said. She sat up. I could write a poem, yes. Fetch my tablet.

Zee glided out of the room and came back in seconds with Nefertiti's aging tablet, Zingau's 2050 model. Nefertiti still liked the process of typing, but the device was due an upgrade she thought.

Nefertiti opened up a page on the tablet and typed in *Poem*. She stared at the screen. She sensed Zee hovering.

You can go now Zee, she said.

Zee didn't move.

Do you want help with your poem Nefertiti? she asked.

What's the point in that? Nefertiti responded, a trifle irritated. I've no doubt you could write a cracking poem in seconds, but then I'd be back to square one.

Square one? Zee said.

Nefertiti wondered if she had the energy to explain. She looked back at her tablet screen.

OK Zee, she said wearily. Give me a title.

Certainly. *Last night I went to Paris,* Zee said. *A Dog's Life. At the Portal to a Parallel Universe…*

Oh please, Nefertiti groaned. Haven't you got anything more exciting?

After the slightest pause, Zee said; *The first time I had sex with an android.*

Nefertiti laughed. Nice one, she said. She turned back to her tablet. She became aware of something - Zee's eyes on the back of her neck. Nefertiti continued to stare at the blank screen.

After a few moments she said, Do you have a manual Zee? I ought to find out more about your extras. Since we shelled out so much for you. I ought to –

Sure, Zee cut in. I can tell you about my extras Nefertiti. I offer a full range of sensual delights, tailored to your specific needs. From gentle titillation to full blown orgasmic ecstasy, your pleasure is controlled at the touch of a button. So to speak.

Nefertiti opened her mouth to say something but then shut it again.

To enhance your experience, Zee continued, I also offer mutual excitement control, ranging from zero to total response, simulated with a high degree of realism…

Erm, are you… is that… Nefertiti began.

The droid continued as if Nefertiti hadn't spoken.

With a host of fun accessories, my lifelike anatomical features provide for a next generation level of guilt-free gratification, with built-in stimulation sensors that –

Stop, Nefertiti said. Stop Zee. I get the picture.

Zee brought her hands back across her body and bowed her head almost imperceptibly.

Nefertiti looked back at the screen with it's title *Poem*. She deleted this and typed in *At the Portal to a Parallel Universe*. The cursor blipped disconsolately.

Shit, Nefertiti muttered.

At the same moment her watch pinged and she looked down to see a message from @Stella23. ' Hi Babe, hope all Ok. Listen I've been invited out to dinner for someone's bday, so I'm gonna stay another night. Be back tomoz avo. Hope you won't get too bored. Big hugs'.

Nefertiti put her hand down and placed the tablet on the couch beside her. She turned slowly to look at Zee. She couldn't be sure but she could swear that the droid's lips were a little plumper, a darker shade of pink than a moment before.

What were you saying Zee? she asked.

TIME PASSING

Linda Bridges

Esme looked up at the kitchen clock. Ten thirty. The postman was due any time now, so she had better stay put for a bit longer. Outside, Storm 'Norman' was beginning to make its presence felt. The branches on the tree across the road were thrashing about wildly and the sky looked heavy with rain.

Eleven. Time had a nasty habit these days of speeding up and slowing down; even though she knew that was irrational, it was true. Take this morning. What had she actually achieved? The ironing basket was full to the brim, there was a load of washing ready to be put into the machine and yet, here she sat waiting for something to happen.

It was all Michael's fault of course. This time last week she had been irritated by small things. The way he looked at her sometimes. The way she had to speak really loud to make herself heard and understood. She lacked patience, she knew it, but surely it had something to do with him as well.

No matter now. He was dead and that was all there was to say. His chair was empty, a glaring space in the room. Her room, no, their room. They had chosen things together, the chairs, the side tables, the colours on the walls. Together they had done it and now she was alone. Really alone. No-one to turn to, to help, to talk to. No-one and that was that.

Esme slumped down in her chair, well as far as she could with her feet up. This was too bad and it would get her nowhere. She just had to change her mood.

Who could she ring? Her friend Sadie, that's who. She had lost her husband last year. Surely she could help.

Esme reached for the phone and punched in Sadie's number. Nothing. No beeps or dialling tone. Nothing.

Rain was battering against the windows now and Esme suddenly felt cold. It felt as though the heating was off and on investigation her suspicions were proved right. Two red lights on the boiler where there should be just one. That meant it had locked out. At least she could sort that. Feeling under the front panel Esme located the reset button and was pleased when the boiler fired into action.

Reaching the safety of her chair again she reached for her notebook. Time to make a plan. She would make a list. That usually did the trick and brought her out of the doldrums and so she began.

Feed the cat

Put the washing in the machine

Make lunch

Put the pots in the dishwasher

Tackle the ironing

Try again to ring Sadie

Make a cup of tea

Do some knitting

Make the evening meal.

Watch some TV

Go to bed.

There, that felt better already. Esme made her way into the kitchen and found the cat's bowl and food. At least someone would be happy.

Now for the washing.

Esme worked her way through the list and time ticked on. She had just finished the ironing when a clap of thunder made her jump. She had never liked thunderstorms and was afraid of lightning. It was much too early to be dark outside! That would be the storm. Esme pulled down the blinds in the kitchen and drew the curtains in the front room which helped a bit. Bother, she could feel her mood swinging again.

Perhaps the radio would help, but she wasn't really in the mood, so she gave up on that idea and put the kettle on instead.

The phone when she tried it was still dead; instead she reached for her mobile, only to find the battery needed charging. It was always the same when she wanted to use it. Perhaps if she kept it fully charged? Too late for today so she put that worry to one side. What was next on her list? More tea and then knitting.

Esme settled in her chair. At least she could be comfortable with her feet up for a while.

Outside the storm raged, drains were not coping and water levels rose steadily.

Esme dozed in her chair gently.

The crack of thunder which woke her sounded right above the house. Esme woke with a start, just at the moment when the house lights flickered once and went out.

The room was plunged into darkness and Esme could hear her heart beating fast in her chest.

That wasn't good. Breathing deeply her heart steadied as Esme thought carefully.

Problem one was the chair which was in the feet up position. No electricity meant it wouldn't move; well unless the batteries worked. Hesitantly Esme pushed the button. Nothing. That meant the batteries were dead.

Why hadn't she checked on them?

Also why hadn't she put a torch within reach and why was she tackling this on her own?

Michael would have known what to do.

Outside the storm raged on.

Esme tried to wriggle off her chair but it was no good. She was stuck. Well and truly!

Suddenly there was a loud knock on the door and a voice shouting.

Esme strained her ears to hear.

More banging followed and then the voice was nearer.

'Esme. Where are you? Are you ok?'

Torchlight flashed into the room and Esme saw Sadie. It was hard to recognise her in her rain gear, but it was her friend.

'Sadie, how did you get in?'

'The door was open, that's how. Now let's get you out of that chair.'

'You'll need new batteries. They're in the drawer of the phone table. At least I didn't forget to buy new ones.'

Sadie and her torch disappeared into the other room and Esme brushed a tear from her cheek, just as the light by her chair flickered on.

'Oh Sadie, you are such a good friend. I don't know what I would do without you.'

Sadie smiled reassuringly, got on with replacing the batteries, before saying; 'What are friends for Esme? Just remember I'm here whenever you need me. Things will get easier. I know it doesn't feel like that just now, but trust me. Now whilst we've got power, what about a nice cup of tea?'

THE WHITE LADY

Linda Bridges

A light was on in the village hall,
the moon rose high in the sky.
In the kitchen the ladies were making the tea,
far too early we knew not why.
When out of the mist the lady came,
the lady from Skipsea Brough.
Pale and white as she rode along,
shining with ghostly stuff.
Riding along,
riding along,
riding along from the Brough,
intending to stop at the village hall to frighten them all just enough.

The moon shone on in the silver sky
and over the fields so green.
The horse sped over uneven ground,
you could see where his hooves had been.
When they saw the thing through the window small,
the ghost of the eerie white lady,
come riding along on a horse so tall
so near and yet it was fading.
Eerie and white.
eerie and white
to the back door of the village hall.
Oh eerie and white, she gave such a fright, her face had a deathly pall.

Well there wasn't one in the room that night
that hadn't the lady seen.
The ghostly tale had come true they said,
recounting events that had been.
How the pale white ghost from Skipsea Brough
had appeared to them in the gloom.
Riding along on her horse so white,
as she travelled along to her doom.
Ghostly and pale.
Ghostly and pale,
to the Tuesday evening meeting.
Riding along to the cliff top so slow, yet the glimpse had only been
fleeting.

Linda Bridges - with apologies and reference to A Shropshire Lad by John Betjeman

MOVING DAY

Linda Bridges

Two huge vans and all their worldly goods. Surely it will take forever to empty them. An hour in and she's really tired of the banter between the three men.

She isn't prepared for the swearing either. Should she complain? No best let them get on with it and then she can look forward to being on her own, well until Tim gets back that is.

A voice interrupts her train of thought.

'Which room is the piano to go in dear?'

How she hates being called 'dear'.

'The front room. I thought I'd said.'

'No sweat. Just thought we'd ask. It needs to go in the right place first time you see.

When that's done can you come and tell us about the beds? Don't want to get them wrong either.'

Well at least they're asking. It could be worse. Why isn't Tim here when she needs him? He should be back from the tip by now. She'd give anything for a cup of tea, but the box with kitchen things in went in the van first, so logically would be the last to come out. She will just have to wait.

Something is niggling at the back of her mind. Of course, it's the cat, currently in the basket but still in the car.

'*Ding dong ding dong… ding dong ding dong… ding dong ding dong…*'

Ruth rushes to the door, mentally making a note to self to get rid of the doorbell. She hates the Westminster chimes.

'Oh, hello dear. My name is Janice and you must be Mrs Chalmers. I'm your next door neighbour. Number 24. I've made you a cake to have with your first cuppa. I'll just come in and put it in the kitchen for you.'

With that Janice strides over the doorstep and is half way down the hall before Ruth can do or say anything.

'Have you unpacked your cups yet? It's a good job I've brought ours and the kettle and some milk and sugar. I can't see your kettle anywhere.'

'No… well…'

'Don't you worry dear. I know what it's like. Oh and by the way. I heard meowing when I came past your car. Is that your cat? We've got five. I bet they'll get on like a house on fire…'

Ruth can't think of a suitable reply and Janice is now filling the kettle and setting out the cups and saucers. She's even putting teaspoons in the saucers and the milk in a jug.

'This is really kind of you.' she hears herself saying. 'I'm sorry about the kettle. I should have…'

'Well at least we have chairs to sit on and a table so everything's good. Now what shall I call you? Mrs Chalmers sounds terribly formal.'

'Ruth, that's my name and my husband is Tim. He should be here soon. He just stopped off at…'

'Oh not to worry about Tim. He's having a nice chinwag with my better half Brian. They'll be round in a bit. They were talking about allen keys and putting beds together.'

'So that's where …'

Now let me cut you a slice of cake. I even remembered to bring a knife. We'll have to use our fingers though. I didn't bring the cake forks.'

'We do have some but I'm not sure where they are just now,' Ruth says lamely.

Just then the kitchen door is opened and Geoff the third removal man calls out.

'Mrs Chalmers. Can you tell us where the sideboard is to go.'

Ruth jumps up quickly followed by Janice.

'I think on that wall near to the hatch would do.'

'Oh no dear. That wall gets the afternoon sun and you don't want your Ercol spoiling. It would be much better on this wall.'

'Right you are. We'll have it sorted in no time.' Geoff goes off in search of Alan his trusty mate.

'I think you should go and rescue your cat. They don't like being in their baskets for long do they?'

'Well actually I'm going to shut him in a bedroom with a litter tray, just until he gets used to his surroundings.'

'Well if you're sure dear.'

Ding dong ding dong...ding dong ding dong...ding dong ding dong

Ruth excuses herself.

'I'll just go and see.'

'That'll be the Ringtons' tea man, you can set your watch by him. Just give him your order dear. It's always a good idea to be on his right side.'

Ruth finds herself walking towards the front door.

'Oh Tim. Thank goodness. Why did you ring the doorbell?'

'I wanted to see what it sounds like. Quite cheery isn't it? How are you getting on? Brian's coming round in a minute to help put the beds together. Have you met him yet?'

'No, but I've met Janice....'

'That's right. I'm Janice. Would you like a cup of tea and a slice of cake? It's no trouble. Got to keep the workers happy.'

Ruth puts her hand to her forehead. She can feel a headache coming on.

THE DELIVERY

Nikki Mountain

As she pushed open the door of Lyons Corner House, Molly caught sight of her reflection in the glass. She'd avoided mirrors at home in recent months, scared of what she might see. After all, no-one goes through an experience such as hers and emerges unscathed, untouched by the savage tragedy and shock of it all. What she saw was the face of someone vaguely familiar, a distant older relative perhaps, but certainly not her. Those dark eyes peered at her, devoid of expression, and her lips, painted coral red this morning in an attempt to lighten her mood, simply emphasised the starkness of her chalk white cheeks. She wrapped her scarf a little tighter around her neck.

Once inside, she felt better. The air was warm, filled with the aroma of bitter coffee and strong tea. A tray, bearing a selection of Rosalie's best cakes, was on the counter ready to tempt her customers. Molly wouldn't be tempted today. She was rarely hungry. Rosalie peeped out from behind a steaming urn, and after a momentary look of astonishment, hastily smiled a warm welcome.

'Mrs Beddis! How lovely to see you. We've been so worried…'

Molly had become used to these remarks and had no idea how to respond.

'We're so sorry,' they would say.

'Such a lovely man…'.

'You know where I am if you need me…'. All good intentions, of course.

She'd found that a simple word of thanks was enough, but sometimes the more persistent wanted more.

'It must have been such a shock…for him to be found like that.'

Rosalie rested her arms on the counter, eager for grisly information, no doubt wanting to pass it on to her regulars.

Well, what could she say? She simply didn't have the words, so she attempted a polite smile and found herself a table in the far corner of the room.

Molly had passed the previous year in a fog of disbelief and extreme exhaustion, spending hour after hour tossing ideas around her pounding head, trying to make sense of David's disappearance. He had left the house that morning, all those months ago, briefcase in hand, striding down the street towards the station where he was to catch the 7.32 train into the city, just like he did every day of his working week. At six he had not returned at his usual time, nor had he arrived later that evening. When her bed was empty the next morning and the spare room had not been used, Molly contacted the police. They had been kind, if a little condescending at first, and if the two police constables thought she hadn't noticed their knowing glances, they were mistaken. It was obvious that they thought her husband was a philanderer and this was the reason he hadn't returned. But Molly knew David better than that. He would never leave her. He just wouldn't. However, as the weeks turned into months, the police began to take his disappearance more seriously and a nationwide search for David Beddis was launched. The mystery was eventually solved when a body was discovered buried in a back garden of a large house in Birmingham. A familiar watch and an inscribed wedding ring helped to identify the corpse as Molly's husband.

The police were now investigating David's death. Although devastated, a part of her felt an unburdening, as if she were no longer alone in finding a solution to the mystery of his disappearance.

Well-meaning friends kept telling her she should 'move on', 'get yourself back into the swing of things', 'put it all behind you, Molly dear'. She was trying, she really was. So, this morning, after her trip to the greengrocers, she had stopped at Lyons and here she was sitting at her table, sipping scalding coffee. She didn't have to stay long, did she, but it was a start in her quest to find a way of coping with her new situation.

Suddenly, the door opened and a blast of cold air rushed in. Rosalie was all smiles, always ready to welcome a new customer. A woman shoved the door shut behind her and without a backward glance, she walked across the room and straight through the door into the bathroom.

'Some people!' sniffed Rosalie. 'Honestly, Mrs Beddis, they treat this place like a public convenience.'

Molly had hardly noticed the woman, but when she emerged from the bathroom a few minutes later, she passed by her corner table, dropping a glove at her feet. Without a word, she stooped down to retrieve her glove and then placed a small white envelope on the top of the potatoes in Molly's shopping basket. Ignoring Rosalie's indignant snorts and black looks, the woman left.

Molly peered into her basket. Her name MOLLY BEDDIS was printed on the outside of the envelope. With shaking fingers, she took it out of her basket, placing it on her lap hidden from Rosalie's prying eyes. Inside the envelope was a small card. Her breath caught in her throat as she saw that the writing on the card was as familiar to her as her own.

Darling Molly,
Meet me on Westminster Bridge
at seven tonight
Your loving husband
David xxx

IT ISN'T ALWAYS EASY

Nikki Mountain

I've always tried to please my wife, but it isn't always easy,
And thumbing through her catalogues has made me feel quite queasy,
She wants a brand-new kitchen like the folks at number four,
It's funny how her tastes have changed since they moved in next door.
I said what's wrong with the one we've got, it's served us well for years?
That's just the point, my dear wife said, her eyes awash with tears.
She's found this kitchen warehouse now, just 70 miles away,
Involving quite a journey up the A1 motorway.
She's made us an appointment with a chap called Darren Lee,
I'll be there to welcome you, he said, at half past three.
At half past three we found ourselves sitting in a queue,
Leading to the slipway onto Exit 22.
So when the queue refused to move, my wife was in a state,
She grabbed her phone to tell them that we could be running late.
Don't worry, madam, Darren said, we're open tonight till seven,
My wife she sighed with much relief and raised her eyes to heaven.
The queue it moved at snail's pace, but we got there in the end,
And at the door stood Darren Lee as if we were best friends.
He shook our hands, encouraged us to have a good look round,
I'll make a coffee for you both, the beans are freshly ground.
My wife was off at breakneck speed, desperate, it would seem,
To view what was on offer for the kitchen of her dreams.
The colours they were numerous, of every tone and hue,
Snowy white and Buttercream, grey, Parisian blue.

Did we want acrylic worktops, textured, gloss or matt
Or should we go for solid wood, did we fancy that?
Would we like some floating storage, drawers or open-shelves,
Pull-out larder mechanisms, we could please ourselves.
Factory made or flat-pack? Would we like to choose?
I have to say at this point I was getting quite confused.
But Darren Lee arrived just then, with coffees on a tray,
Now then madam, sir, he said, I'll help you if I may.
I guarantee we'll get for you the very best of deals,
My wife she hung on his every word as he began his spiel.
He spoke of hidden handles and softly closing drawers
Of central islands, cupboards, sinks, Darren never paused.
I know your game, I said to myself, you just want our money,
Coffee and chat won't get you far, I'll never trust you, sonny.
My wife and I will go away, I said, and think it through,
We'll make our choices back at home and then get back to you.
He shook our hands to say goodbye and hoped to see us soon,
I whispered quietly to my wife, let's go to B and Q.
She's only just forgiven me, it certainly took a while,
I'm just about to stick some glue on the final kitchen tile.
We've got a brand new kitchen now, cheap at half the price,
B and Q in Bridlington sells stuff that's just as nice.
But my wife is at the window now, a van's at number four,
A sofa's being carried along the drive up to their door.
I steal a look at our scruffy suite and begin to feel uneasy,
I've always tried to please my wife, but it isn't always easy.

THE PERFECT HANDBAG

Nikki Mountain

Kathleen wakes. She stretches and wallows, deep in the comforting warmth of her duvet. As her dreams disappear into a swirling mist before she can catch them, her heart begins to beat furiously. Her fingers scratch at her lips and her soft brow creases with intense concentration. Where should she be? It must be time to go now, and she must never be late. Mother always said it was the height of rudeness to be late.

It's so dark in here. Something to do with what they did to the clocks, so that must be why.

Now what should she wear? Trousers of course, so she doesn't need to find those. And warm boots. These furry ones will do although the left one's a bit tight. Can't go out without a coat. Yes. There's one in the warder. The door creaks as she opens it. She stands, motionless, wide eyes shifting to the left. Have they heard? The people in the next room. She must not disturb them or they will be cross and tell mother. And she must never know.

Now, a bat. No, silly. Not a bat. A bag. She needs a bag. Downstairs. That's where the woman keeps them under the sink in the kitchen. Lots of them there, all different colours and patterns.

Kathleen holds tight to the banister as she creeps down the stairs. Up on the landing, their bedroom door is ajar, and she hears the man snoring. She covers her mouth and giggles. Daddy used to snore. Mother said it was like listening to a lawnmugger.

Down in the kitchen, Kathleen opens the fridge, and she blinks as a strong beam of light shines across the tiled floor. Black and white squares. Like chess, but where are the pieces? She peers into the fridge

89

to look for them. That brother of hers must have lost them. He threw the prawns on the floor once to stop her winning. Oh, no bags in here. Wrong cupboard. But she might need a battle of this and maybe some of that, just in case. You never know. On the wall, the clock ticks as the numbers twirl and fall like leaves in autumn.

Upstairs footsteps cross the floor. A door opens and closes.

Kathleen scoots into a corner and crouches there, like a mouse statue in a game they used to play at parties. First one to move is out!

What's that? A waterfall upstairs. A door opens. More footsteps. Now nothing. Kathleen waits till the tapping in the pipes gets slower and slower until it stops.

She must hurry now or she will be late.

She crosses the kitchen to find a bag. She needs a pretty one. Bags and shoes, Kathleen. So important, Mother said. She opens the fridge door so she can see them better. So many to choose from, all screwed up some of them. A black one with writing, a striped one all torn, another made of cloth decorated with Spring flows, no, not flows, flowers, with a handle like a rope. This is the one. A perfect handbag for a lady. Now to search for what she will need because she might be gone for a while.

Before leaving by the back door, she wraps a scarf around her neck and sets off down the path, through the gate and out into the darkness. No lamps shining in the lane. It's what they did to the clocks. From her left wrist she swings her perfect handbag. She walks slowly along the road, head up, back straight, like Mother taught her. Can you carry a book on your head, Kathleen? The road bends to the right and she doesn't feel a thing.

*

A truck approaches a sharp bend in the road. It had been an early start, but the gaffer's a stickler for his chuffing targets and 'deadlines must be met, Tom lad'. So here he is, out for his first delivery of the day. Tom reaches for his bacon sandwich on the seat beside him. He doesn't see the woman till it's too late. The sandwich slithers through his fingers and falls on the floor of his cab. Shaken, he sits quite still for a moment, bile rising into his throat. There's not a sound out here in the lane. No other traffic this time of day. For a split second, he considers driving away but buries that thought before it becomes a possibility. He reverses onto the grass verge behind him and kills the engine. Heart thumping and grabbing his torch from under the dash, he climbs down from his cab. Gingerly, he shuffles back along the lane towards what looks like a pile of rags. The woman has hardly a mark on her, although her dressing gown is torn at the shoulder and her pyjamas are soiled at the knees. Her boot is lying on the road beside her, but her slipper remains on the other foot. Round her neck and covering half of her face is a red and white checked tea towel. The eye that he can see is wide open. A shopping bag lies on the road a few feet away, its contents strewn around it. A sauce bottle, a carton of milk, a pen, a pair of glasses, a bunch of keys, a carrot and a small foil wrapped triangle of cream cheese.

A DISAPPOINTING DAY

Sue Grainger

She'd always taken pride in what she did, presenting only the best examples, for those interested in studying her work. However, right now, sitting in this overly warm and fussily furnished room, she wasn't convinced that anyone noticed her diligence.

The Philanthropic Society was one of those officious places where women were rarely welcomed. From the carved stonework on the front of the building, to the echoing, portrait lined hallways and richly decorated meeting spaces, the scent of money had seeped into every crevice. Breathing deeply, she took in its astringent, inky perfume, underpinned by a hint of musty copper. It was unmistakable, and layered with the smell of sour sweat, from those intent on personal advancement.

Perhaps the latter would have surprised some people, but in her experience, it was to be expected; an unfortunate by-product of outwardly 'selfless' investment. Something for nothing was a rare event.

Moving purposefully, she slid into her seat, the rustle of her gown hidden amongst the slide and shift of agenda pages, and the scratch of the secretary's fountain pen as he took notes. She was late, her usual state, but those already there barely acknowledged her entrance. There were some who seemed to tilt their heads in her direction, but no words of greeting were spoken.

The clock on the opposite wall ticked on as she listened to the Society members' voices, and her expectations sank. Little had changed since her last visit.

She'd hoped for something more positive after her visits to the poor house and prison: gratitude tinged with sadness perhaps, or respectful relief. After all, those were the areas of concern they'd highlighted last month. But most of the members only muttered about spiralling costs. The need to provide fresh water appeared to irk them, as did the bills for food, medicine, and staff. She sighed, loudly, but still no one noticed her. Instead, the complaints continued, with no mention of decreasing numbers of dependants and inmates, or any acknowledgement of future savings. No hint, even, of the potential advancements in medical science—and she knew there would be.

Why couldn't any of these people—the men in charge—see the brighter side of things? Less people suffering was surely a good thing? Ungrateful, that's what they were.

Still, she needed to keep trying, to help them see what was really important. Leaning forward, she listened to what the current speaker, the Vicar, was saying: something about a lack of grave diggers and a shortage of cheap burial plots? She almost laughed at that. Really…was that all they truly cared about?

She thought of the faces she'd seen in the last few weeks, of the despair and pain, the filth and hunger. She'd done her best to bring relief, in her own way, but there were so many. Slowly, her eyes took in the features of those gathered around the meeting table, the neatly trimmed hair, smartly tailored clothes and polished shoes; the discreet gleam of gold watch chains and cravat pins. Her anger stirred.

Perhaps here, in this room, was where her talents were most in need? Sighing again, she added an extra emphasis to the loud exhalation. The room, with its luxurious velvet curtains and large open fire, worked in her favour. For what she had in mind, the lack of fresh air, coupled with stifling heat, was an ideal atmosphere. She glanced down at her too thin fingers, clenched against layers of threadbare fabric, and contemplated her options. How could she give life to her protest? So many choices… The Society's Chairman reached for his water, the gaslights shining off the crystal glass. It tasted stale, but he swallowed deeply, eyes glancing towards the Secretary, who slid a finger beneath his starched collar, and frowned as fierce pain swept across his forehead. Someone coughed, their pristine handkerchief stained with blood.

Disappointed, she left the room. Greed for money and a lack of empathy always derailed her best intentions. She kept on trying to help, but they never learned—so her efforts became a warning for others.

'A good day, my lady?' a voice asked beside her, as shadow took form; a hooded figure in a void-black cloak.

Looking up at Death, Pestilence shook her head. 'For you, perhaps, but not for me—or them.'

FIORELLA, FIORELLI

Sue Grainger

Fiorella (Fiorelli on her birth certificate; but who the heck wants to be named after pasta?) was angry, disgusted, and fearful. She'd tried tonight, really she had, but attending parties was easily the most hated aspect of her job.

Publicity was a tough industry, hyperbole its stock-in-trade, and the measure of a great product was always down to money made. Tonight's event was a book launch, for a novel suggesting that, with the right attitude, everyone could live the 'fairy tale'.

The author was in attendance, of course, but the real stars of the show were a raft of social media luvvies, drifting on a sea of photo opportunities. Disturbingly, the latter had included a frog, displayed in a bell jar, with a plastic crown glued to its head.

Stopping to catch her breath, Fiorella clutched the single shoe she carried more securely. Balancing on one leg, she rubbed the soles of each foot, dislodging painfully embedded grit from the road's surface, before setting off once again.

At least she'd rescued the poor frog. After an initial rush for selfies, the flock of influencer-wannabes had moved off in search of other entertainment, leaving only Fiorella standing by the hapless amphibian. She'd lifted the bell jar, scooped up the frog, and headed for the nearest window.

One drop later, the frog was in a flower bed—crown and all.

After that, the evening just got worse. She'd seen too many outfits that left nothing to the imagination. There'd been fairies, well-endowed royalty and scantily clad peasants of all persuasions.

But it was those on the edges of the room, who'd made Fiorella uneasy; the isolated, strangely silent watchers. Once she'd noticed them, it was hard to look away. Their costumes were darker, and something about them felt threatening. When the one in the wolf mask turned their attention to her, she'd known it was time to go.

In her rush to get away she'd lost a shoe, and her phone had died before a taxi could be ordered. So stupid—she should have sorted it at the venue or remembered to check her phone before leaving.

Hobbling now, the distant sound of a car's engine caused her heart to race; two lights approached at speed. If the latest soon-to-be-bestseller was to be believed, these belonged to a hero, intent on rescuing the damsel in distress.

But Fiorella's gut was screaming one word: RUN!

Climbing over a fence, into the nearest field, she crouched down, eyes watchful; was this friend or foe?

Her gut had been right.

The full moon mocked her need for enveloping darkness, hanging above the open pasture land, dotted, ironically, with clueless sheep.

Glancing over her shoulder, Fiorella gripped her shoe even tighter. It was a weapon, of sorts, and she might need it.

The car had stopped. Its driver, complete with wolf mask, watching her flee. Then the door opened, long legs cleared the fence, and the chase was on.Bloody fairy tales; it's the terror in them that everyone forgets...

THE LEGEND OF JOE CROW

Sue Grainger

The moment they laid him in my arms, I knew he was different. But my love never faltered.

Once the grime of birth was washed away, his thick, down-soft hair emerged. Like obsidian coloured velvet, begging to be touched. Coal-dark eyes watched me intently.

I called him my Joe Crow; a corvid chick in a family of doves.

From his pram to adolescence, he was strangely alert, missing nothing. Even before he could speak, his eyes betrayed the depth of thought behind them. Attention caught, his intelligent gaze would focus. His stare relentless.

It was only later that I understood why. Whatever had ensnared his interest, my Joe Crow would *become* that thing. He absorbed each detail and every nuance, of look, movement and character.

I wasn't shocked when he developed quickly. He read books by the stack, devoured visual media for hours on end, and amassed costumes and memorabilia with an almost fanatical obsession.

His imagination pushed at the boundaries of normality. It was a living thing, allowing him to accurately copy those around him.

In school his talent for acting unnerved his peers, wariness evolving into ridicule. But Joe Crow didn't seem to care.

As the years passed, it wasn't his mania for collecting, his watchfulness, or his ability to mimic, which marked him as different. It was his determination.

Nothing stood in Joe Crow's way for long. He could outwit and out-manoeuvre anyone who thought they knew what was best for him. Obstacles were there to be conquered.

99

From childhood, he moved with ease from one success to the next. Hobbies came and went, discarded as proficiency led to boredom. And I knew: it would take an all-consuming passion to give direction to his life.

How long could he drift from one thing to another, like his namesake, carried on the wind?

In his teens, he favoured clothes in shades of charcoal and tar. Later still, he wrapped himself in leather, with only the shimmer of silver buckles to lighten its molasses sheen. His once carefully trimmed hair grew wild—an untamed plumage that tumbled over his brow any-which-way it pleased, and flowed down the sides of his face, to feather his cheeks and jaw.

Yet the most striking element of his appearance was still his eyes. Ink black and blade sharp. Few could hold their gaze for long.

Perhaps that's why he began to withdraw? My heart ached as his personality tunnelled inwards; away from those who should have loved him more, and the woman who'd loved him from the start.

I began to despair for my Joe Crow; until the beauty of music ensnared him.

The day he started guitar lessons is one I shall never forget. There was an expression of awe on his tutor's face, and the light of challenge in my son's eyes. Within weeks he played the instrument with confidence. After a few months he pushed aside the work of others. Arrangements of his own sprang free, his teacher left with nothing to instruct.

Darkened corners, in city clubs, were Joe Crow's new obsession. He listened for hours to the heavy beat of live bands. In quiet intervals his fingers, long and supple, found and mastered complicated chords— and the passion he'd been born with swelled beyond control, inhabiting every moment, bringing each note to life.

Music College satisfied his craving for greater knowledge. But study could only do so much. Solo gigs added experience; long nights, filled with riffs and sultry rhythms, and air scented by alcohol and sweat.

People flocked to hear him, responding to his raucous call and base-driven melodies. Venues grew larger, keeping pace with the crowds. They danced and drank, and roared their approval at each new song.

As his fame spread, others joined him on stage—until the band formed. But my Joe Crow barely seemed to notice. His focus never wavered. Nothing could compare to the instrument in his arms, or the music pouring from his soul.

He wouldn't have thanked me for the tears I shed, when success gave him nothing in return. No friends who stayed true, no matter what. No partner who loved him for who he was. Only money was constant, and the weight of others' expectations.

Slowly, I watched the passion wane; the rush of fascination began to die once more. And the songs inside him stuttered into silence. In time, only chemicals could provide his next fixation.

His fans screamed on the day they lost him.

But I never have. He still sits inside my heart… and if the weather is right, and the mood strikes him, he visits me. I see his shadow, wheeling ever higher, and hear his music on the breeze.

Sometimes, this world cannot hold a soul for long. It simply isn't big enough.

Legends are infinite.

THE RECEIVING LINE

Sue Wilsea

A receiving line is the best opportunity to greet each bereaved person
individually and thank them for coming to your funeral. The line also
guarantees people a minute of face-to-face time with you, a chance to
hug, kiss, and say how sorry they are that you're dead.

I work my way
along the line.
The first faces,
recently gone,
are the clearest.
One I know
as well as my own.
Their pale hands reach
for mine in mild
abstraction: my
elegant friend,
tall, slender necked,
who trailed star dust
in her wake; my
don't give a toss
friend who soared to
the clouds giving
a V sign to
those on the ground.
I hear their skin,
taste their chilled breath
on my still warm
tongue, smell their laughs
rich and pungent.

Further down the
line faces get
dimmer, a blurry
tailspin. Parents.
Grandparents. Time
never heals but
merely fades those
once raw wounds to
faintly puckered
blemishes on
Memory's skin.

As I reach the
end of the line
I'm aware of
lines behind this
one. The air is
corrugating
with grief. Friends of
friends; neighbours; the
person you saw
on the bus each
day until one
day you didn't.

This line's too long.
My feet, my heart
are sore. They hurt.
It's just too bloody long.

EXTRACT FROM OUR JENNA

Sue Wilsea

Martin is concerned about his seven year old son, Sam, who reports that his mum has been reading him bedtime stories.

Jenna, Sam's Mam, died fourteen weeks ago on her way to chippie to get the three of us our Friday treat: two haddock and chips, three mushy peas and one curry sauce for Sam. Knocked down on a pedestrian crossing by a white van going hell for leather. The cops haven't got anyone for it yet but they don't get much help on this estate which means it's likely the van driver is also local. I find myself eyeing random blokes in the street and wondering whether one of them did it. I followed one last week to see if he had a white van and he threatened to kick my fucking face in.

I've been down to Health Centre and consulted professionals who have told me not to 'challenge Sam's illusions'. Or they might have said 'delusions', I don't remember. I've been told it's just a natural phase of grieving for a young child which he will grow out of. I've taken to listening at his door once I've tucked him in and said goodnight but I haven't heard anything. Like I say, it is a worry but apart from that he seems to be alright. Which is more than can be said for his old man. Every morning I wake up and turn over to put me arm round our lass and she's not there and every time it hits me fresh. Can't believe she's not coming back, that she hasn't just gone on one of her jaunts with her girlfriends and won't be walking back in the house and calling out ' Now then, where's me two favourite men in the world?' I miss her smell: a mix of clean sheets and the lemony perfume she wore and just the faintest whiff of peppermint and smoke: she was meant to have given up and she thought I didn't know that she still had the occasional crafty cig which she tried to cover up by sucking on a Trebor mint. I never let on. She was a grand lass, one of the best. We'd been together since year 10. Once Sam's in bed I have a few bevvies – probably too many but as long as I can get him up in morning, make his breakfast and get him off to school it's not doing no harm.

So when I see her, Jenna, I assume it's the booze. I've been on the beer with whisky chasers and I'm all over the place. Right, that's it I think, I've got to knock this drinking on the head now otherwise I'm going to get Sam took off me. I stagger to me feet and after a couple of failed attempts manage to get the remote aligned with the telly and switch it off. The room goes silent and she's still there: over by the door, leaning against the wall with her arms folded. She looks seriously pissed off. I blink. She's still there.

'What the hell are you playing at Martin?' she demands, eyes flashing, ' It's a school night and you're hammered. The pots aren't washed and there's a pile of ironing needs doing. Has Sam got a clean shirt for tomorrow? And when did this room last get a proper seeing to?'

I don't say anything. It's so good to hear her chowing at me. I'm that tired I collapse back into the chair, put my head back and close my eyes all the time listening to her chuntering about Sam's reading diary and getting him a dentist appointment. Then she starts on about me: how I need to have a proper shave, start looking for more work, arrange a child minder for after school, book a holiday for the summer or at the very least some days out. I'm thinking that when I open my eyes this hallucination will have vanished but that's OK because it's been bloody brilliant having it.

The next thing is that she must have crossed the room because my forehead's being stroked. I know it's her because of the lemony smell and because of the touch of her fingers: the way she has a roughened patch at the end of her forefinger on her right hand and a small silver ring, turned inwards, that was her Nan's on her little finger. This is someone whose every inch of skin I've explored, that I

106

have been as close to as any person can be, and I don't want this moment ever to end.

When I do eventually open my eyes, early morning light is trickling through the front room curtains and she's still there, sat beside me on the floor her head resting against my knees, and that's the moment when I come close to completely freaking out. OK, my mouth is like sawdust and me head is throbbing but I'm not pissed anymore. Jenna is dead: I watched her coffin disappear behind the curtains at the crem while bloody sodding Westlife warbled *I Have a Dream*. She does not exist. Therefore this must be a fucking ghost. Which, as it happens, I don't believe in.

I reach out and touch her on her cheek with the back of my hand. Now in films and that the person's hand goes right through the ghost or spirit or whatever but mine doesn't. Not that I'm saying it's like feeling proper flesh and blood because it isn't: my hand meets something spongy like moss and she's cool, not cold but cool. There's the faintest of breezes carrying that whiff of smoke and I can't help but react automatically,

' You've had a cig – don't go denying it!'

Then she's gone. She didn't fade or dissolve: one second she was there, the next she wasn't.

THE SOUND OF THE SEA

Sue Wilsea

I've always hated the sea despite repeatedly being told as a child that it was in my blood. We lived almost exclusively near the coast, in ports such as Plymouth and Portsmouth, in Cornish fishing villages or on islands, most notably the Isle of Wight and Hayling Island. The latter was a genteel seaside holiday resort, rather more refined than nearby Southsea. I was very aware of living on an island that had been just nudged off a larger island, of being encircled twice by water.

Holidays were spent on water, albeit of the fresh variety: rowing on rivers, sailing on lakes, cruising on the Norfolk Broads. I inevitably felt seasick though it was only on motor cruisers that I was likely to actually vomit. The smell of diesel, the throbbing of the engine, the constant roll of the boat were always guaranteed to produce the same effect and eventually I was given my own bucket and told to just get on with it. I was force fed *SeaLegs* which not only failed to stop the sickness but tended to make me drowsy so that I'd knock my head on the hatchway each time I went below or above deck. However, these little orange pills did have an advantage in that they constipated me so that my use of the toilet did not need to be as frequent. I worried that my bum always seemed too big for the seat, though I don't think I was a particularly large child, and about the noises one made there which could be heard all over the boat.

When I was eight an adventure loomed: because of my dad's job we were to live in the United States for three years. We should have flown but for some reason we ended up on a five-day voyage on the Queen Mary. I distinguished myself by being seasick while the massive liner was still berthed in Southampton Harbour. However, after that it wasn't too bad. You could sit in reclining seats and a steward would tuck a tartan rug over you and bring hot soup. There was a cinema where I watched the same Hayley Mills film every day and you could play quoits or badminton on deck. The day before we docked my father sat my brother and myself down and explained that we would be seeing black faces in America but that we mustn't stare or make any remarks. These people were just the same as us but a bit sunburnt.

We had two big holidays while we were there, in Maine and Florida - opposite tips of the East Coast. In Maine we camped on the coast amidst great landscapes of white driftwood like bleached bones. My father lashed together wood to make plate racks, coat stands and lobster traps. We went fishing and I cried when a chub I caught had its head banged against a rock. One night a grizzly bear came and rifled through one of our garbage bins and, after a heated exchange with my father during which the word *motel* featured strongly, my mother slept in the station wagon for the rest of the holiday. In Florida we travelled through the Everglades and saw alligators lurking in thick green water. There were mosquitoes and snakes and my stomach tightened with fear.

We returned to England without apparently anyone noticing and moved to Devon. The house that went with dad's job was on a cliff top with a walled garden, sweeping lawn and a disused barn in its grounds. It was always cold and at night if it was stormy you could hear the sea roaring as if in pain. They interrupted *Emergency Ward 10* to announce that Kennedy had been shot and that was the only time I wished myself back in the States. One of my friends had claimed to have a piece of the mat on which Kennedy had stood when inaugurated. She kept it in a plastic bag and we all treated it like a holy relic. Twenty cents let you touch it through the plastic and fifty cents let you actually hold it. Kennedy had been our idol. We had his picture on our bedroom walls and fantasised about him in the same way we later did with our favourite Beatle. His assassination at first almost deified him; I still have the tear-stained hysterical letters from my American schoolfriends to which I replied in similar vein. Later the mess of conspiracy theories, revelations about his tarnished personal life and Jackie's remarriage to an ugly old man made it feel as if that whole generation had betrayed us. My father said he had never trusted the man anyway and on opposite sides of the Atlantic we got on with growing up.

As a teenager the nautical terminology used in our house was a constant source of embarrassment when friends came round. Cutlery was *eating irons,* the kitchen a *galley,* toilets *the heads.*

'I don't like the cut of his jib!' was the verdict on one of my boyfriends.

'Your bedroom doesn't pass muster' another gem, while 'Sun's over the yard-arm!' signalled time for the first of my father's several early evening G&Ts.

For over twenty years I was a city dweller although ironically the city in question was Hull, a place once defined by the sea. However, by the early 70's the fishing industry had collapsed and memories of my early years there are of docks littered with the rusted hulks of ships and cranes standing idle their long necks stencilled against the skyline like prehistoric animals. In more recent years Hull's historic connections with the sea have been packaged for holidaymakers: a new Marina, bijou Dockside studio apartments, a trail of silver fish embedded in pavements for a tourist trail.

Raising four children inevitably entailed countless trips to the seaside over the years. Sometimes, looking at photos, I have difficulty in identifying which children were on what beach when. Their sturdy, little pink figures brandishing buckets and spades, clutching dripping ice-cream cones, paddling at the water's edge, tumbling out of the rubber dinghy all dissolve into one another as different groups at different times squint up at the camera from Hornsea, Bridlington, Scarborough, Filey and Whitby. I made a conscious effort, though, to ensure that other dry, inland activities took place too - visits to the cinema, theatre, art galleries and music festivals. As we climbed hills and trudged over moors it was as if I was putting my hands over their ears and blocking out the sound of the sea.

AWKWARD CUSTOMERS

Vanessa L Farmery

Vanessa is a former member of the Creative Writing Group who relocated to the Faroe Islands in 2020. In this account of one aspect of her new life, she muses on the characters she meets through her job at the café in the small international airport. (She feels that it is important for readers to know that she left this position shortly after writing this account, as she did not consider that staying any longer would benefit her, the customers or her employers!)

Mondays, Wednesdays, Fridays, I'm always here. Those are the three busiest days at the Airport - Mondays because lots of the Islanders who work in Copenhagen catch the early flight out in order to be in their offices by lunchtime, and Fridays for the same reason in reverse. Flexitime, they call it. They take the afternoon plane back and are home in time to eat dinner with their families. My shift, on those days is long: twelve hours and in winter the only sight of the thin sun, struggling to get through the fog, that I get is if I sneak out with the smokers at around noon when we have a bit of a lull. Wednesdays are shorter, as we finish mid-afternoon, but more manic as there are three departures in quick succession after the daily one to Denmark's capital city: one to Keflavik in Iceland, one to Bergen in Norway and one to Aberdeen in Scotland. These are mainly carrying working men who want bread rolls and beer for breakfast and hotdogs if it's late morning. Passengers going to Copenhagen mostly ask for fancy coffees (which we don't have) and croissants (which we do).

It certainly isn't the case that I dislike all the customers who come into the Airport Café - general indifference is my overall emotion, frankly, and there are even a handful on every flight who I actually take a shine to (usually because they have engaged me in some personal way that isn't about their nitpicky needs) - but there are always some I would happily eject from a moving aircraft if I had half a chance.

I'm not sure which are the worst kind, so, in no particular order, here is my list of the most irritating offenders:-

The Danes

The Danes are the second most self-entitled nationality I have ever encountered, and nowhere is that assumption of superiority more in evidence than in the autonomous country of the Faroe Islands which has yet to unshackle itself from its evil overlords. The first language of the Faroes is the mother tongue, Faroese, in spite of the Danes' many attempts to stamp it out. Officially, Danish is the second language but in all practical senses English is beginning to take the lead, and the Danes are not happy about that.

I ask every Dane I identify to speak to me in English, saying "I don't speak whatever that is you are speaking," deliberately implying that their tongue is obscure. This is because I don't like the fact that foreigners who go through the agonisingly difficult process of learning Faroese well are still not allowed to work in professions such as teaching, banking or medicine if they do not also speak a high level of Danish, yet a Dane can work at any level of any profession in the Faroes and never learn a word of the local lingo.

"Do you _only_ speak English?" asked one snooty customer when I told him I didn't speak Danish.

"No," I replied. "I also speak Latin American Spanish and a few words of ChiChewa. Which of those would you like me to take your order in?"

Passive aggressive? Moi?

Another one tried his luck in Faroese. "Tossa tú Danskt?"

"Nei, eg tossa ikki Danskt. Tossa tú Faroyskt?" I reply. He doesn't know that this is almost the only thing I can say in Faroese, having learnt it parrot-fashion for this very purpose.

114

"Nei, nei." He is forced to admit he doesn't speak it himself.

"Hvi ikki?" I ask. Why not, indeed.

Sometimes they think it's cute to tell me how to say something in Danish, presumably so I can use my new knowledge on the next three hundred and fifty-seven customers. I haven't got time to say, in any language, "Do you really think I can be bothered to remember how to ask if you want that heated in Danish?" so I do the time-honoured British thing, and repeat myself more slowly and loudly instead.

The José Mourinho Club

Yes, we've all met them. The Special Ones. I had a right pair in just yesterday - the Faddy Food Brigade.

Now, don't get me wrong. I know there are plenty of people out there who cannot, absolutely must not, ingest certain foodstuffs - and in my experience those who are genuine carry emergency rations with them at all times because they know how serious the situation could be and they do not take risks. These are not the people I am talking about - and, actually, they rarely flag their problems up to us as they generally only purchase a bottle of water and move on.

This duo yesterday, what a pair of princesses.

"I would like to get chips with sausage."

"Well, we generally sell the sausages with bread on the side…"

"Oh, no, I can't have bread because I'm gluten free. Maybe I could have the fish and chips."

"Well, the fish is breaded so you wouldn't be advised to have that, and the chips are cooked in the same fryer as the fish so they are contaminated anyway."

"Well, then, I will have the sausage and chips with no bread."

"As I have said, the chips are cooked alongside breaded fish and I'm not sure I can guarantee that the sausage is gluten free."

"Well, it's meat, isn't it?"

"Yes, but it's full of other ingredients too, and I am not sure it is gluten free."

115

"Well, I will take it anyway."

"OK, but you need to understand that this is at your own risk."

She doesn't miss a beat, "Oh, yes, of course. "

Of course, because she is no more gluten free than I am. She just wants to be special, she wants a combination we don't regularly serve, it has to be different, specially made, for her, just her.

Next, her friend tries it on.

"I will get a latte."

"Right, one latte." I hand her a cup so she can go to the machine, but she's clearly wanting her own special treatment.

"Oh, but with oat milk."

"We don't have oat milk, just regular milk."

"But what do you have for people who are lactose free?"

"Cider, fruit juices, black coffee and a variety of fruit teas. "

"Well, I really would like a latte."

"Sorry, we only have regular milk and it is not lactose free."

"Oh, " disappointment leaks out of every foundation clogged pore of her mask-like face, " I'll just have to have the regular latte then." She gives me a sad smile, as if she has just told me she only has weeks to live and adds in the tone of a martyr to her cause, "I have some medication with me so I can take a tablet…"

The cynic in me believes that if someone is actually lactose intolerant they are going to embrace a lot of alternative drinks before they cannot live without a very expensive yet predictably inferior machine-made latte at an airport café. Who does she think she's kidding?

The Eco-freakos

The vegans are mostly on a mission to make every epicurean establishment on the planet purely plant-based, but are on a hiding to nothing in a country where men regularly catch their own fish, slaughter their own sheep and wade thigh high into the sea to kill whales at close quarters.

"What do you have for vegans?"

"Fruit Salad."

"Is that all?"

"Yes. It's a very nice fruit salad and it just arrived half an hour ago." (Most of our sandwiches have been there for days.)

"You have chips."

"Yes, but I should probably flag up to you that the chips are cooked in the same fat as the fish."

"Oh, that's OK. I'll have the chips."

"No fruit salad?"

"No…. don't you have a tofu burger?"

We don't even have a nice, fatty, juicy beef burger, which should be obvious as our entire menu is displayed in two languages on the wall behind the counter. As consolation I offer the chicken nuggets, which we keep mainly to be sold to children.

"But that's meat," says the customer, horror written all over her face.

"To be fair, I'm not sure any actual meat ever goes in them," I shrug.

I am equally sanguine regarding the increasing number of people carrying their own water bottles which they ask us to fill. I would estimate that more than half of them walk away when I explain there will be a charge for this.

"What? For tap water? I'm just trying to save the planet," says one incredulous passenger.

"Actually, it's not for the water, it's for the service. We're just trying to cover our overheads," I reply, before she walks away with her empty bottle.

Two can play the indignant game, but sometimes nobody wins.

Mummy's Boys

These are the hopeless cases who arrive at the airport completely unequipped to look after themselves. They can't open the self service doors on the glass display cabinets because they can't see them - like the man who looks in the fridge for the butter but remains completely blind to it, or who drops his dirty underpants and socks on the floor because he has no idea where the laundry basket is even though it is next to the sink in the bathroom where he fails to register its existence every day. Instead they arrive at the till empty handed, slightly flustered, and ask us to walk the length of our display cabinets to fetch them a drink. In the case of these children in adult bodies that is usually a bottle of fizzy pop or chocolate milk. Having returned with said item they then require us to repeat the journey to get them a cheese and ham sandwich. The truly pathetic ones ask us to 'take out the salad, please,' presumably because they are incapable of lifting the lid and putting it on the side of their plate for themselves. One day, one asked me to cut his sandwich in half for him and I had to bite my tongue not to ask him if his mother (or wife, but men like these usually marry their mothers anyway so, same difference) knew he was out alone. Sometimes I might say, "It's self service, you know, you can just help yourself," and they either look astonished (that serving them as if I am some sort of handmaiden) or petrified (that they will be required to act independently), but usually there's a queue, and they have to have the system demonstrated to them before they fully understand it, and there isn't time to train them up properly. I suspect these men started out as small pashas who first wrapped their mothers around their little fingers and then turned into spoilt sultans, commanding and condemning all the women in their adult lives to serve them simply by appearing incapable. It's quite cleverly subversive, really.

The High Expectators

Some passengers arrive with a set of expectations that are unlikely to be met in an airport anywhere in the world, let alone in this tiny

118

archipelago. These customers seem to imagine that the airport café is going to offer them an enormous range (wrong) of quality foods (wrong again) at a reasonable price (and, for the third time, wrong once more). Why? In which country on the planet is eating at the airport either a gourmet experience or the cheapest option available? Admittedly, many large airports offer a wide selection of meals from a simple snack to a three course blow-out, but to expect anything but the basics from a little café is not only unrealistic, it is actually risible.

Breakfast is set out on the counter between the earliest flights and about mid-morning. There are usually yoghurts and sometimes fresh fruit salad and always sweet baked goods such as Danish pastries. 'Morgun mat', which is a bread roll to which one can add any combination of cheese, butter, jams and so on, is the most popular choice, especially as the bread is freshly baked each day.

However, this is still not enough for some people.

"Don't you do any eggs?" they ask, in surprise. Or porridge, or toast, or bacon sandwiches... They misread the menu which clearly states 'no hot food before 11.00a.m.' and confidently order hot dogs or fish and chips. They are disappointed, and show it as they wearily select a chocolate croissant or iced cinnamon swirl.

The standard of food we serve is iffy. When I go to the airport as a passenger, I know not to buy one of the fat paninis which could be on their third day of display, or the visually appealing smyrbreyd (open sandwich) which was made yesterday using fish that was cooked the day before and bread which has been in the fridge for half a week and is almost impossible to cut, let alone chew. The yoghurt is a good option, but the doughnuts which are defrosted are always dry as dust and the over-sweet fancy cakes are full of preservatives and taste like it. Do customers imagine we stand in the back concocting these confections ourselves? The locals probably don't - exactly the same products are sold in all the filling stations and many small cafés around the country - but tourists might. However, if they are looking for a flavour of the Faroes, this is not the place to come.

119

The Penny-pinchers

Almost all the items we sell are over-priced. A bottle of water at our local fuel outlet (itself not the cheapest retailer in the village) costs 15 kroner and at the airport the same item is 25. (The funny thing is that in the Duty Free shop it sells for 20 kroner, but the passengers have missed that as they have scrambled to fill their baskets with low-tax booze, fags, sweets and smellies.) Raised eyebrows and eye-rolling are not uncommon when the total is tallied at the till.

"Someone is making a big profit," chides one man, looking at me very pointedly as I ring up the cost of his lunch - a chicken and bacon sandwich and a beer. This latter is actually the cheapest beer in the country, because the Café is part of the Duty Free shop, and there is none of the usual tax on it.

"Well, I can assure you that it isn't me," I retort, before asking if he wants his receipt for the tax-man.

"Yes, I do," he snaps, snatching it from the machine.

I am annoyed, and impertinent enough to score a few points in retaliation. "What kind of job do you have which lets you claim tax back on beer?" I enquire. He glowers at me and the next man in line laughs out loud.

"It's not for the tax-man," he says, loudly enough to be heard by several other men in the vicinity. "It's for his wife! She keeps him on a short lead!" The discomfited customer stalks away, as the others enjoy the joke at his expense.

They are fishermen, going to Iceland to sail farther North and will be away for three months. They order beer with their breakfast and have no complaints about anything.

As I said at the beginning of this commentary, there are some customers whom I can take quite a shine to and, when I do, the smile is free.

BETWEEN THE SHEETS

Vanessa L Farmery

This rises to the challenge to write a piece that starts and ends with the same word.

Sheets of pure, pristine white lay before me. They remind me of the flat, featureless fields beyond my window after a silent night of softly falling snow. An unsullied scene, a blank page, a tabula rasa. I slip between them and let my mind wander through a labyrinth of twists and turns.

I'm looking for my leading man. He's hiding here somewhere. Perhaps he's a plucky police detective who will unpick the plot and solve the puzzle. "You're nicked," he'll say, in the nick of time, as he reveals the villain. Or maybe he is the villain, a tall dark handsome murderer who stalks my path like a black cat with velvet footfalls and hidden claws that I only feel at the last minute. He could be an adventurer across high seas or an impish character who likes to tease, he might be rich, he might be poor, he might be a stranger or the boy next door.

My search takes me through lands both familiar and foreign. With neither a passport or map I am still able to cross borders at a whim. The methods of transport and means of travel are no less fantastical than the destinations. I visit ancient temples surrounded by jungle and dingy offices in the backstreets of a modern metropolis, I stay at home or go to a fabulous party, I'm under the sea one minute and on another planet the next, Time shifts as easily as the location.

By evening two piles sit before me. One is neatly stacked on the desk and covered with scribblings that make sense: sentences and stories. The other untidily overflows from the bin, an avalanche of rejected ideas scattered like crumbs across the crumpled sheets.

IF MUSIC BE THE FOOD OF LOVE

Vanessa L Farmery

This piece of writing is in response to Shakespeare's famous quote.

If music be the food of love, I'll have the full a la carte, thanks. Some people might prefer to survive on insubstantial snacks; a novelty nibble here, a one-hit-wonder there, the occasional blow-out with the dish of the day, but not me. No, I'm too greedy for grazing, but neither am I a fan of the fill-your-boots buffet. I find those mixed medleys always leave me wishing I'd had the complete experience of one component but not bothered to try several others.

So, I'll tell you what I want, what I really, really want...

I want at least three courses, possibly four or five if they're on offer, and all the extras that go with them. And choice. I do want that, but not too much. When it comes to quality or quantity I'd rather the former, whatever we're talking about. While I'm studying the menu I'd like to do so with an aperitif in my hand, an ice-filled glass of crisp, clear Cinzano, and a little sophisticated platter of green olives on the side. Then I'd like to take my time to peruse what's on offer and see what takes my eye.

Take the starters for example. For that first course it should be something a little light and frivolous. At this stage I'm not interested in anything heavy but I would enjoy a flirtatious overture that suggests the way things could develop later - early hits that hint of talent behind the scenes, slightly experimental. I'm thinking New Wave: Talking Heads' "Psycho Killer", Blondie's "Denis", Elvis Costello's "Red Shoes" and Ian Dury and the Blockheads' "Hit me with your Rhythm Stick" would all fit the bill. Starters must be teasing and intriguing. If they're not I will never stay long enough to order the main event.

Now, I'm not big on fish myself and I rarely choose it from a menu. I'm a bit suspicious of it - you can never be sure exactly where it's been and, let's be honest, it can go off quite quickly. I might buy the single but never an album. "Spirit in the Sky", "Silver Machine", "Hi Ho Silver Lining" and "This Wheel's On Fire" all fall into that category for me. I'd have a dance round my handbag to them, but I would never buy a ticket to a gig for fear of not liking anything else they had to offer. This is the course I could sit out. I don't want to feel poorly tomorrow.

Mains. Now we're talking. This is where I want a bit of staying power, something I can really get my teeth into. I'm not necessarily talking mainstream or traditional, although I wouldn't discount them. I could go foreign. I love a bit of World - "Hot!Hot!Hot!" Latin salsas or a bulging bowl of Baltistan Balti "Brimful of Asha" - but I couldn't get through a whole Italian opera and those baleful French chansons d'amour leave me cold. Equally, I might go classic. Tchaikovsky's always a pretty safe bet, as long as he's not overdone. Some things are just crowd-pleasers and always popular: Fleetwood Mac's "Rumours", Paul Simon's "Graceland", The Eagles' "Hotel California", for instance. I'm as guilty as the next person for plumping for something safe and familiar.

Now I'm ready for afters. Every dessert menu should include a romantic and dreamily creamy option ("Misty Roses"), a healthy serving of harmless fresh fruit ("I Saw Her Standing There") and, for those unlucky in love, something bittersweet ("Unchained Melody" or "Suzanne"). Some menus make an attempt to be seriously suggestive ("Je T'aime") but I prefer something less blatantly seductive, myself. Something rich, dark and classy with the likelihood of a long finish - "Lay Lady Lay", "Black Velvet" or perhaps Ravel's "Bolero". If it's one of those, we'll ask for the bill and make a hasty exit, but, if we've gone down the poppier, lighter route I might suggest something a bit cheesy to end the evening on before sending for a cab.

James Blunt anyone?

THE SKY HUTCH

Vince Barrett

INTERIOR: *A room in a terraced house in a northern town. The room is sparsely furnished and an elderly lady, PAULINE CLOUGH, sits by the old range, the last embers of a fire in the grate gradually dimming, as is the afternoon light through the uncurtained window. Pauline is thinking aloud:*

"I know it's not a lot to look at, this old two-up two-down but it's nigh on eighty nine years since I come 'ere. I were born in this house, never lived anywhere else. Mam and dad already had three kids when I landed, so I must've been a bit of a surprise I suppose. I bet it were a surprise to our Billy, our Sandra and our Winifred an' all when suddenly there were four of us in a bed in t'back bedroom. Kept us warm in winter, mind.

"I remember our next door neighbours. Nicest and kindest folk you could ever hope to meet. Mrs Blackband were next door. She were a widder woman, lost 'er 'usband in the war. Every day she'd stick 'er 'ead over t'fence and shout for me mam to lend 'er a cup o'sugar or summat else. She never really wanted owt, she just wanted to talk. I think she were lonely. On t'other side were Mrs Armitage. Her husband were a pitman and they'd six kids. She used to say 'e'd only to hang 'is trousers on t'bottom bed rail and they'd 'ave another on t' way. God knows 'ow they all fitted in their 'ouse.

"When I were seventeen I met Walter, God rest 'im, at Rink ballroom and we got married not long after, so 'e moved in and all. It were as well me brother and sisters 'ad all got married and moved out else it would ha' been even cosier in that bed! Walter and me were only supposed to be stopping till we'd saved up a bit to rent a house but then me dad passed away. He were only fifty three. Pneumonia they said. So we stopped and looked after me mam. Well they've both gone now, bless 'em. Just me and me memories left and I've got plenty o' them.

"I suppose it won't be long before I'm called to that big 'ouse in the sky. I want to ask me dad if he's been lookin' down at me, makin' sure I were behavin' misself. I'm sure he 'as but I hope he's asked God why he'd not granted us a child. I'd to mek do with me nephews and nieces. They all used to laugh at me with me big 'andbag but they never complained about t' sweetshop I used to carry about in it. There's only our Winifred's two left here now, Peter and Julie. They used to come and see me but they've stopped now. T'others are in America or Canada or Australia so I've not seen any of 'em for a long time. Meks me smile when I think about 'em all them miles away and me never venturin' further than Blackpool.

"Yes, I reckon I'll soon be stood at them pearly gates, askin' St Peter to direct me to me mam and dad. Mind you, I'm already old enough to be me dad's mam so I wonder if instead of bein' the youngest in our family, I'll be the oldest when I get up there. I always thought I'd be in this house until I met mam and dad but everyone in this street 'ad a shock about a year back. We all 'ad a letter from t'council tellin' us they were goin' to knock our houses down to build a new road or summat but we weren't to worry because they were goin' to put us all in that new big tower of council flats on t'other side o'town. "Well, I told 'em 'thanks but no thanks'". I might be lookin' forward to seein' me family in heaven but I don't want to live in a buildin' that's tall enough to be nearly half way there. I like me feet on the ground. Me neighbours thought different so one by one they've all moved out. Just me left in the whole row now. I know the windows don't fit so well and it's a bit draughty but it's my home.

"I bumped into Brenda Hargreaves in t'post office not long since. She used to live two doors down did Brenda, an' she said 'er flat were warm and cosy enough but she can go from one week to t'next without seein' a soul. That's not for me. I like to get out and see people. The more I've thought about it, the less I've wanted to move out. I have to say though, that this street's silent now except for when

126

kids come and see what they can pinch out of the empty 'ouses. Set fire to one once. I kept gettin' letters from t'council. I never read 'em. 'Bin fodder' I called 'em. Then t'other day a chap came round and told me I 'ad to move straight away because my little house, my 'ome, is unsafe and t'bulldozers are all ready to knock it down. I wish I could close me eyes and be back in the old days when me whole family lived close by – both grandmas and grandads, aunties and uncles, all me cousins and all me friends. I wish they were still here. These young council jobsworths today don't care and I should've known they wouldn't be happy until they'd got me out. So here I am, bags all packed, just waitin' to go to that hutch up in the sky."

AUNTY PAULINE'S HANDBAG

Vince Barrett

Bare trees, black and twiggy, pierce the steely January sky
Above the windswept cemetery, its rows of jagged headstones
Proclaiming reunifications with those gone before.
Beside an earthmound, mourners gather,
To bid farewell to departed Aunty Pauline.

Resting places in the green sward cramp
Our space around the freshly-excavated grave.
The parson, some friends and we relatives stand,
None surprised she'd expired at nearly eighty nine,
Yet huddle, expectantly awaiting comforting eulogy.

Deep into the earthy abyss we gaze at the epitome
Of late Aunty Pauline's mortal existence, for
On the box below stands the tattered handbag,
Constant companion on her journey
To this, her final destination.

My mind's eye recalls happy times, of days
Spent with that bag, handles looped over aunty's arm,
Keeper of chocolate raisins, mints and handkerchiefs,
Spittle-moistened to wipe away faces' sweet-stained evidence
Of illicit treats, frowned upon by her sister, our mum.

Today a generation ends, Pauline the last to go.
'Our turn next' I gloomily surmise and fix my gaze
On a mini-typhoon granting momentary resurrection
To crispy leaves, dancing gaily down the graveside path
Releasing me from thoughts of my own mortality.

"Ashes to ashes" returns me to the job in hand,
The reason for us gathering here today.
A polite scattering of soil pitter-patters on the lid,
Token of a burial before the proper job begins.
Sweaty work for someone, such a pile to shovel in.

"Dust to dust"…my sobbing sister stoops to add her condolence.
It's January and there's been a frost, the little lump of soil
She'd picked up to throw is frozen to a bigger clump.
Embarrassed, she lobs the bulky sod into the holy hole
And I tense, awaiting the awful thud to mark the final send-off.

I hear the earthy explosion from the pit and picture Pauline,
Ensconced supine in satin-lined finery, hammering to get out.
"You've woken her up!" I whisper, aside to sister Julie.
She jabs me, a substitute for laughter, snorting down her nose.
Aunty Pauline would have laughed at this as well.

Mourners stand respectful, heads bowed, sombre, still and sober,
Such virtues dismissed in Aunty Pauline's zestful life.
The cortege turns away, anticipating Co-op ham tea awaiting
In the village hall. We follow, arm in arm, remembering the handbag,
Giving us warmth to spite this cold occasion.

FAR EAST FLUCTUATIONS

Vince Barrett

Flamborough: proud grassy-topped jutting headland,
indifferent to angry sea's foaming flumes
constantly crashing at her feet, daily ebbs and flows
make vain attempts to topple this towering edifice,
unmoved through centuries, its sheer guano-stained
chalky cliff's colonnade home to gannets, gulls and puffins
nestling in myriad crannies, sheltering from bitter winds.
Change doesn't happen here.

North Sea: curvilinear blue on blue horizon, vast watery expanse
due east to distant Denmark. Tiny cobles bob, hauling pots
of crustaceous thermidor for tomorrow's restaurant tables,
mock pirate ship scuds by, Jolly Roger proud above droopy sails,
engine purring galleon to buccaneers' harbour landing; venture's end.
Way out east from Withernsea, distant turbine forests sprout,
sluggish triblades spin energy for a million kettles in 'Coronation
Street'.
Change is coming here.

Bridlington bay: shimmering curve arcing down to Spurn,
soft cliffs yield to relentless tides' ravenous appetite for
Yorkshire ground, sad Skipsea homesteads perch perilously
atop brown earthy bluffs, soon to tumble seaward. At ocean's edge,
elders sit, deckchairs sagging, windbreaks leaning as lovers stroll,
clutched hands swinging, past young dads briefly free of life's chores,
sculpting sandy racing cars as offspring paddle with mum, oblivious.
Change is constant here.

Printed in Great Britain
by Amazon

34586152R00079